A SPOONFUL of SUGARPLUMS

Other Books by C. L. Fails

So Okay...Treasured Stories from the Life of James M. Robinson, Sr.

My Magical Story Journal

The Secret World of Raine the Brain Series

The Ella Books Series

The Christmas Cookie Books

C.L. FAILS

A SPOONFUL of SUGARPLUMS

A CHRISTMAS NOVEL

LaunchCrate Publishing
Kansas City, KS

A Spoonful of Sugarplums
Written by C. L. Fails

LaunchCrate Publishing
Kansas City, KS
info@launchcrate.com
www.launchcrate.com

Ordering Information:
Quantity sales. Special discounts are available on quantity purchases by corporations, associations, and others. For details, contact the publisher at the email address above. Orders by U.S. trade bookstores and wholesalers.

Library of Congress Control Number: 2019919267

Hardcover ISBN: 978-1-947506-15-2
Paperback ISBN: 978-1-947506-16-9

Printed in the United States of America
10 9 8 7 6 5 4 3 2 1

First Edition

For those of you in search of seeds of hope, may you find them and plant them for others to discover as well.

"I wish I could tell you that it all ends well. Unfortunately we won't know the answer until all is said and done."

Table of Contents

TABLE OF CONTENTS

A SPOONFUL of SUGARPLUMS

Chapter 1
Dr. Chris

"I wish I could tell you that it all ends well. Unfortunately we won't know the answer until all is said and done."

A thick air of uncertainty hung heavy in their hospital room as I asked if there were any other questions before nodding and confidently walking away.

It was the absolute worst part of being a Doctor. People come to me because they want answers. People come to me because they need hope. But sometimes, the best I can give them is the truth and pray that they find the seeds of hope that are embedded within it.

Seven year-old Marley had been my patient for just under 6 months. She had the biggest smile, the kindest heart and the warmest spirit I have ever seen. Given the battle she was facing, I knew that her optimism would come in handy. I looked forward to swinging by her room the most as I made my rounds at Hope Gardens Children's Hospital. Each child added something unique to our wing, but Marley was a different kind of special. You've met them before I'm sure, the kind of person who made everyone's day brighter just by being in the room. That was young Marley.

You can imagine now, just how hard it would be to potentially be responsible for dimming the light of a shining star like her. I held a strong faith in her ability to find the smallest glimmer of hope through the weeds of uncertainty. Her life, and maintaining it, would be dependent upon it.

Above the stillness of the hospital hallways rang an announcement that echoed from chamber to chamber.

"Paging Dr. Chris. Dr. Chris to the Family Room. Paging Dr. Chris. Dr. Chris to the Family Room."

I walked with purpose towards the Family Room. This was the holding space for families of children who were visiting the hospital.

Approaching the family room, I slowed my pace to ensure that all families would feel a sense of calm as I entered. I caught a glimpse of the family that was awaiting my arrival. Two parents worked to distract a young boy who might have had some misplaced bones in his arm; yep broken ones.

The Family Room attendant introduced me to the family as I walked in the room.

"Dr. Chris, this is the Williamson family. Williamsons this is Dr. Chris." The young boy, through his pain, looked at me with confusion on his face, a common occurrence when families are given my name without me being present in the room. I don't know if it was my curly afro that threw them for a loop or my pecan colored skin. Either way, I was face to face with the same amount of befuddlement as I receive in every similar situation. And just as I have done in each of those situations, I adjusted my glasses, tucked my clipboard under my arm, extended a hand to the woman of the family, looked the child in the eyes with a smile on my face and nodded to any other friends or family who were present.

"How are we doing today?" I asked with a manner of concern.

His mom, fighting back tears because of the

pain her child was in, could only shake her head from side to side and mutter the words, "we've had better days, haven't we Jax?"

I could see the tears welling up in her eyes, but wanted her to be strong for her son. Placing a gentle hand on mom's shoulder, I turned towards Jax, "Should we get you to an x-ray machine so we can see just how good you got it?"

He nodded and chuckled before answering with a raspy, "Yes."

"Great!" I turned to his family members, "Which of you is going to be Jax's strength while we take a look at his arm?"

His Dad volunteered to stand with him and promised to send regular updates to Jax's mom. So we took a stroll by the Christmas tree and its twinkling lights.

"What are all of those birds on the Christmas Tree?" Jax asked with the same curious look that framed his face when the Family Room attendant introduced us to each other. We paused for a moment so I could show him one in detail.

"THESE are wishes for the children who are staying with us in the hospital. Some will only be with us for a short time. Others though, stay with us for much longer. The birds are peace doves, and they carry messages to help plant seeds of hope. Do you see those bumps in the paper?"

"Uh huh," his weary voice replied, still ripe with curiosity.

"Those are wildflower seeds. So every year after the Holidays pass, we gather each wish and hold them in a special place until Spring. Then we plant them in the garden outside."

It was the first time I heard his father speak, "It's a literal Hope Garden, Jax. I think we must be at the right place huh?"

I gave a reassuring nod to his dad, and glanced at the sparkles in Jax's eyes. "When we're all done with your arm, would you like to leave a wish for someone who'll be staying a little longer?"

"Yes!" he emphatically replied, his chest swelling with pride, "and maybe mom would like to write one too, Dad."

"I bet you're right, Bud," he affirmed while patting Jax on the head and thanking me with a smile.

"Okay, well we better get to it so we can get you back here to leave your messages." I started walking away from the tree and motioned for Jax to follow. "Green or Blue, Jax? Which color is your favorite of the two?"

"Umm..." he paused, deep in serious thought. "Green!"

"Perfect! You and Dad, meet me in the Green room. I'm going to grab a couple of friends to help me out and I'll be right in, okey dokey?"

"Okey dokey," Jax affirmed.

My x-ray tech did a phenomenal job grabbing the scans we needed to show Jax and Dad the resulting trauma, while our Social Worker found out exactly what happened from both Jax, and mom. Then I came in, set the arm and we got him all wrapped in a cast that we all signed with holiday wishes. While Jax was resting, I placed a dove with a wishes for a speedy recovery on his bedside table and signed it Dr. Chris. I also made sure to leave a few empty doves for his family to complete.

With Jax all taken care of, my attention turned towards Marley. I gazed out the window while recalling the words I had so carefully chosen to say to her and her family. Her surgery was tomorrow and it weighed heavily on my mind. I ran through the options available, seeking confirmation that surgery was the best choice in this situation. I couldn't see another choice. This was our best fit for attacking the tumor that had been plaguing her health for the last 6 months. I inhaled deeply, taking in the view of the couples and families who were enjoying the sights and sounds of the holiday season. Christmas lights and holiday carols sprinkled warmth in the cold air of December. Kansas City was a great place to live, but it was particularly charming during the holidays.

It was nearing the end of my shift so I completed one more round, visiting my patients, reading holiday themed bedtime stories, singing songs with and to the children, and leaving them with sprinkles of hope for the dawning of tomorrow. I wished my staff a good night then dashed out to my car to avoid the chill in the air, humming all the way. Because I had picked up someone else's shift, I was leaving a bit later than usual. It was my favorite time of year, but I felt like I was missing out on all the festivities. Mom had invited me to trim the tree, but I was working. My sister had invited me to go ice skating with her family (niece and nephew included) this weekend but I was scheduled to speak on a panel.

Before heading to the house for the night, just to turn around and do it all again tomorrow, I hopped over to the Fresh Grind Coffeehouse down the street. They were serving Hot Cider, and Hot Cocoa to the people out enjoying the holiday season. Jumping in line while looking up at their menu wasn't the wisest idea I've had, but it was one that certainly changed the trajectory of my life. I bumped into someone and caused a chain reaction of falls akin to a set of dominoes. During the rest of the year, there would've been a bunch of grumpy people sifting for their belongings through the pile of cold-weather gear. But because it was the holiday season, everyone simply picked up their gloves and earmuffs from the floor, laughing all the way.

"Oh!" was the only thing I could muster as he grabbed me, keeping me from smacking my face against the floor. I was so embarrassed.

"Whoa there. Are you okay?" he asked as I gathered my gloves and composure like all the other customers.

"I'm so sorry," I muttered, still not looking up.

"You're fine," he said. *Definitely not looking up now,* I thought while contorting my lips into an uncomfortable half smile. He stumbled over his words, "I mean, I'm, you're, you're okay."

Just as awkward as me, this one. I averted my stare from the floor, looked him in the eyes and smiled, "Thanks. I think."

There was no reply, but his gaze stirred a part of my soul that I thought I had officially closed down for the season.

We nervously chuckled and inched closer to the front of the line.

"I just made that really awkward," he spoke in a sultry voice, awakening the butterflies in my stomach. "Let me buy your..."

"Apple Cider with a spoonful of sugarplums. Thank you, but I should be buying your..."

"Same," he said with a quizzical look on his face.

"I thought I was the only person who liked Sugarplums," I said to the stranger.

"I come to this coffee shop because it's the only one in the city that I've found who serves cider with sugarplums."

"Me too." *Odd.*

We had inched to the front before I knew it

and the barista asked us, "what can we get the two of you tonight?"

"Oh, we're," I started.

"Just here to get two of the city's finest hot apple ciders each with a spoonful of sugarplums," he finished.

I looked at him, then back at the barista and nodded, asking for an extra dash of cinnamon extract in one of them.

"Both of them," he added.

"We'll have that right up for you!" chirped the barista.

We inched around the corner towards the register with the rest of the line. The sounds of the brewers roared in the background and the patrons in front of us seemed to have forgotten about the domino tumble I had started. But I could not. I stood beside this ridiculously handsome man that I had literally stumbled into, agonizing about what he must have been thinking about me and my two left feet. We didn't say much else to each other, but I had a lingering feeling in my gut that I knew him. I didn't understand it but I was leery to say the least. By the time we reached the registers, our piping hot ciders were waiting, steam rising from the cups like something from a movie.

"Hey, Charlie!" the cashier gushed. "I should have known these apple ciders belonged to you. Must be a long night of grading if you're getting two!"

"Hi Oakley," he chuckled. "Actually, one of these belongs to..." he handed one of ciders to me. I forced a smile at Oakley, raising my eyebrows quickly.

"Oh, well," Oakley replied with a shrug of indifference. "They're on the house," Oakley finished, expeditiously moving on to the next customer.

Odd, I thought, grabbing a handful of napkins to cut some of the heat from the cup. I turned towards the door, looking for this Charlie character to say thank you, but he wasn't there. I turned to my other side, still no Charlie. Just as I was about to chalk it up to a Christmas miracle and leave, I heard someone clear their throat from behind me. Instinctively I jumped, preparing myself to throw some hot cider on someone. Fight or flight is a real thing with me. Thankfully for him, I caught a glimpse of disappointment on Oakley's face before I became a twirling tornado of cider. She didn't know it, but she had just saved Charlie from becoming a walking ad for the Fresh Grind. Instead I turned slowly, simultaneously raising my cup in thanks and nodding in Charlie's direction, "Thank you for the cider."

"Thanks for bumping into me," he said raising his cup my way.

I muffled a chuckle and suppressed a smile, leaning towards the door so he knew I was on my way out. I saw in his eyes that he was going to ask me to stay, so I steadied myself to respond.

"So listen, I'd love to learn more about the person who created the first coffee chain... reaction."

He was a charmer. I had made a resolution to steer clear of those types years ago and well, my word is my bond, so it's never been broken yet. "I really would love to share more with you, but I was rushing in to grab a cider on my way home from a long shift, and-"

"Oh, so you probably want to get off of your feet. It looks like there's a table opening up over..."

"There is, yes. I see it. But I really do need to run. If there were a drive thru here, I would already be on my way and-"

"We never would've had the chance to bump into each other. Literally. I understand."

"Thank you for the cider, Charlie..."

"You're welcome...???" he paused, waiting for me to insert my name.

"Great, hope to bump into you here again!" I piped up.

I hit the door so fast you would've thought I had just robbed the place. My heart was pounding, my breathing sped up on me, I wanted to look back at the door of the coffeehouse to see if he was watching, but at the same time I was terribly afraid that he would be.

As I drove home I hoped beyond hope that I would see Charlie again, but I didn't know him from Adam and it was late at night. Like, late, late. I needed to get out of there. Plus, there was still the matter of Marley that I was focused on. I had a million excuses why I needed to go, but as I entered my yet to be decorated condo, and slumped into my comfy spot on the couch, I couldn't help but wonder what might have happened if I chose to stay. There I sat, in my feelings until I drifted off to sleep, rising with the sun the next day.

I headed back to the hospital after a full night of rest, and dreams about the mystery man named Charlie. I was determined to let him go if I didn't see his face today, and considering just how busy my day was, I knew that it was highly unlikely that we'd bump into each other again.

Marley's was the first face I saw that morning. She was chipper and yet she seemed a bit worried. I sang to her as I swung my head in her doorway, "Are you ready?"

"Yes, I'm ready!" she sang back to me. And poof, the worry wrinkle that had stretched across her forehead all but melted away.

"What questions do you have for me today, Marley?" I wanted to ensure she didn't go into surgery worried about something that she didn't ask.

"Dr. Chris, what happens to me if I don't wake up from surgery?"

Working at a children's hospital, I've received this question a lot over the years. Typically it's asked out of curiosity. This was the first time I've been asked by a child who genuinely did not know whether she would survive the surgery.

She had so much resolve in her face, like she was okay with whatever the outcome. So when I told her, "that all depends on what you believe," she smiled at me. It was a knowing smile, as though she'd already spoken with someone that told her what was on the other side.

She held my face in her little hands, looked me in the eyes, patted my cheeks, and whispered, "I know you're going to do your best and the rest is up to God."

I nodded and affirmed that I would. Then we crossed pinkies to promise each other that we'd both give our best; me during surgery, and her holding onto hope after surgery was complete.

Her parents came in to sit with her before it was time for us to transition to the operating room. I asked the same question of them, "What questions do you have for me today?"

They shook their heads in dissent. There were no questions they wanted to ask. Not in front of Marley. I wanted to give them time together, just the three of them. So I shared that, gave them a final rundown of the timeline and headed for the door of Marley's room. When I got to the hallway, I felt a hand on my shoulder. It was Marley's father. He shook my hand, thanked me for caring for Marley throughout the last few months and asked me for my genuine thoughts on her survival of such a risky surgery.

The last words I muttered to him were the same as what I shared yesterday.

“I wish I could tell you that it all ends well. Unfortunately we won’t know the answer until all is said and done.”

I looked him in the eye and told him that I would give 100% to Marley during surgery, but the 24 hours that followed were going to be highly critical for us to watch. Part of her survival rested on whether or not she held hope of staying in this world with us. He nodded, his eyes swelling with tears until they could no longer hold them, spilling out onto the linoleum of the hospital hallway.

“I understand your concern, pop. She needs your strength and optimism. Let us do the worrying for you.”

He nodded, gathered himself and returned to the room with a bright smile.

“What did you ask, Dr. Chris, Dad?”

“I just thanked her for taking care of my little girl and giving her best so she has an opportunity to grow up into a young lady."

Hearing the hope he had just delivered to Marley, I walked down the hallway to my office to gather my thoughts and composure.

When the time for her surgery arrived, I prepped our team, reviewed our game plan for surgery, post op, and recovery, then scrubbed in. We followed the plan methodically, and midway into surgery hit a speed bump. Marley's heart rate bottomed out. She flatlined. I closed my eyes, tilted my head back, and took a deep breath to steady my nerves. With my head still tilted back, I opened my eyes again and there she was. I was looking Marley directly in the eyes.

Her little hands cupped my face, patted my cheeks and whispered, "I know you gave your best. Remember, the rest is up to God."

I exhaled, looked back down at the table and there she was, resting peacefully while the rest of the team was talking over each other as they worked their hardest to revive her. I was overcome with peace and asked them all to be still and breathe. With all of the chaos stopped, I rested one hand on Marley's heart, looked up at the clock in the Operating Room, and waited.

I don't remember much after that but I do

have a fleeting memory of crying with Marley's family, and returning to my office chair to sit in solitude for a while, only to have it broken by a knock on my door.

"Dr. Chris? Dr. Chris?"

It was Jax's mom, coming to let me know that they were on their way home.

"Thank you for taking care of my son."

I stood up to shake her hand and instead was greeted with a hug. Jax, popped into my office and handed me three doves to place on the Christmas Tree; one wish from each member of his family. The one with Jax's handwriting was addressed to Marley. I felt a large lump in my throat but was just able to push out a thank you in his direction.

They were discharged from the hospital and I stepped away for a quick reprieve and a much needed meal. Nothing fancy, just some warm soup to fill my belly on this cold December Saturday. There was always my old standby small diner on the corner. The Fresh Pantry never failed me. I could see from the window that my trusty corner booth was even open. It gave me a great glimpse of the entire cafe as well as the passersby on the street. I ordered my

Vegetable Soup and plopped down in the booth, letting all of my angst seep out as I sunk deeper and deeper into the plush seat. While I waited for my soup and bread to be delivered, I took in all of the festive decorations. Regardless of the season, The Fresh Pantry, always went full throttle in the decor department. I felt like I had been transported to a holiday wonderland. I was greeted by a wreath at the front door, garland lined the bar top and escorted me back to the booth. There were metal toy trucks and vans carrying Christmas Tree's on their roofs at every table, and ice skates wrapped with red ribbon, hung from every other window pane, poinsettia wreathes in the others, and twinkle lights, those twinkle lights were everywhere. Before I could finish taking in all of the decorations, a bowl full of steaming soup was slid on the table before me. A plate underneath the bowl carried two warm, soft, buttery, homemade breadsticks. *They win again.*

I had been escorted to an alternate reality just long enough to forget the tough morning I had just finished. Marley's surgery was one I won't soon forget. It's highly likely in fact, that I'll never forget it. The world of pediatrics was just as tough emotionally as it was mentally. Thank goodness for spaces like The Fresh Pantry and colleagues who know the journey. Before I knew it, both of those worlds had collided. In walked

Marlo, one of the other doctors from Hope Gardens. While I didn't think I was interested in seeing anyone from the hospital, this was a welcome surprise. Marlo knew exactly what I was experiencing, having had a challenging surgery last month. He made his way back to the booth and asked if he could have a seat.

"Please do," I replied, urging him with a hand gesture to have a sit down across from me.

"How are you, Chris?" he asked, his face holding concern.

"It was a tough morning, but I'm going to be okay," I followed. "This soup is helping the stress melt away," I said between spoonfuls. "What did you order?" I was an expert at dodging the tough conversations, at least the ones I wasn't fully ready to have at the moment. I had done that last night with Charlie, the mystery man - speaking of whom I just so happened to see walking in the direction of the coffee shop where I met him.

I couldn't tell if he saw me or not, but I definitely saw him. Then I was reminded of what I'd told myself this morning, before Marley's surgery, before Jax was discharged, before taking a dip of reprieve in this warm bowl of soup, "let him go if you don't see him today."

Well there he is. Thanks, Universe.

Chapter 2
Charlie

I ended the school day the same as I did every Friday, with a timely message to my students, "It's Friday! Forget all of this week's challenges. Relax, have fun, and..."

"DON'T SEND YOU ANY EMAILS!" they all replied with laughter.

"Stay safe so I can see you on Monday!" I finished.

They rushed out of the classroom like a herd on the run and I exhaled deeply as I waited for the class full of 4th graders to empty completely. My work wasn't done yet as I still had a responsibility to ensure they got to the bus safely, which meant they would first have to wait for the walkers to grab their belongings and be escorted off of school grounds. While we waited, a dance contest ensued and became far more serious than any elementary school dance off should ever be, ESPECIALLY on a Friday. So I did what any self-respecting educator would do. I joined in to get them to stop. My versions of today's dances weren't even close to resembling how they were supposed to look. *Sorry not sorry, kiddos. This bus riders line is moving out the door and you're all the most important part.*

"We have ONE MORE WEEK before the Holiday Break, Mr. Hughes!" So much exuberance filled that sentence. I couldn't possibly let them know how I really felt about the week before the break and the overly sappy, Christmas festivity filled weeks that would surely follow it.

"You're riiiiight! You must be excited!" I said, feigning interest.

"See you on Monday!" the last words I heard as she hustled out the door.

I peeked outside and noticed that the dance contest had been reignited, and who was leading the charge? My best friend's child, Jax. He had taken the competition to an entirely new level, adding aerial moves to his arsenal of dancing.

I hustled to the door, and hollered in his direction, "Jax, keep it safe!" He waved goodbye and hopped on his bus. I pulled my cell phone from my pocket and called his house.

"Hey Steve, Jax is on his way home. He's got some dance moves, man." I paused, listening to his Dad talk about how much more active he had been recently. "Uh huh, he did do a couple of flips. One of them was off of a bench," I chuckled. "I mean listen, I've seen these same moves from someone else. If my memory serves me correctly, I think you flipped up and over a wall in college to catch Sabrina's eye."

Steve had a wild streak before Sabrina, but she calmed him down. He was much more respectful as a result of her presence. The level of disrespect Pre-Sabrina was ridiculous though. You wouldn't even think he was the same person. I on the other hand, may have stopped him from busting his head open a few times after realizing that it was probably at my prompting. Call it a guilty conscience or whatever. I miss the old days, the days when Christmas meant hanging with the guys at the ice skating rink, with absolutely no desire or intention to get on the ice. What we were hoping for was to find our people, or at least a placeholder to keep us busy. One day it was friendship as usual. Then there she was, Sabrina, and Steve's life shifted. She was good for him, and I was happy for the two of them, but I missed not having my own Sabrina. Sure I was a knucklehead, but that was all for attention. Aloud, I asked the Universe for my own person and suddenly she was right there in front of me in the form of Sabrina's best friend, Cheryl Watkins. At least that's what I thought. Maybe it was my optimism that led me to believe that one set of best friends would meet, date, and marry another set of best friends. While that would be ideal, it was not realistic. The truth is, Steve and Sabrina worked. I on the other hand forced a relationship with Cheryl, that I knew deep down was not going to work.

We dated through college and when I graduated, I moved to another state where we would be forced to try a long distance relationship that I already knew was doomed to fail. Did I tell you that I avoid conflict like the plague? Yep. I don't like it. Cheryl was a good woman and I was not surprised to learn of her marriage to another man, about two years after our relationship had dissolved. I too had moved on, to another city in fact, from Jacksonville to Chicago for another corporate opportunity. Meanwhile, Sabrina and Steve had a child and settled into life in Kansas City, where she was raised. I visited them often, especially at Christmas, and had the chance to watch Jax grow up, albeit mostly from afar. I grew to like Kansas City. Big town amenities with a small town atmosphere and feel. Of all the places I visited, it felt more like home than even the place where I was raised.

Watching Jax grow up was all the impetus I needed to reconsider my career track. The corporate world was great and all, but I felt a nagging urge to do something other than make money. I used to have regular flashbacks of my time with literacy summers in college. That's where I felt like the work I was doing mattered. Connecting with the children, encouraging their love of literacy, if there was a way for me to become a teacher, I would gladly take on the challenge. At the time I was dreaming about it, I had no clue that I would actually have the chance to do just that.

It was during one of my Christmas visits to see Sabrina, Jax, and Steve, that the shift occurred. We had spent the day ice skating (yes, I was actually on skates this time), shopping, and taking a tour of the Christmas lights that helped set the city aglow. It was so much fun watching Jax's excitement, that I was actually looking forward to Christmas, in spite of the fact that I was still rolling solo. We stopped into a coffee shop to thaw out and get some hot chocolate and there she was, Oakley Powell. Oakley, the woman who would end up ripping my heart out after I took a leap of faith and moved to Kansas

City to give my dream of being an educator as well as our relationship a shot.

I signed a 3 year contract with a local school district that would give me both the opportunity to earn a Master's degree in education, and three years to hone my craft in the classroom. Before the first full academic year was up, Oakley, had decided that she liked me better when I had a fancy well-paying corporate job. She didn't want to date a teacher. But instead of telling me all of this, she started dating someone else while we were supposed to be exclusive. I was actually on my way to pick up her Christmas gift (a ring), when I saw her all hugged up with some other guy in the very jewelry store where her engagement ring was waiting. Talk about a swift punch to the gut, and the roundhouse that followed? Her laughter and totally unnecessary extra squeeze of her boo, that followed my visible confusion. Maybe I deserved part of that for not being honest with Cheryl. They talk about Karma being swift and I guess it caught up to me.

So here I am, a year later, teaching 4th grade and dreading Christmas. I wasn't ready for that flashback, but it's not uncommon for me to have them. The good news is, I have come to realize part of what Cheryl might have felt. Even though I knew the way I treated Cheryl wasn't right, I didn't have an inkling into what that might have felt like. Shortly after the turn of the new year, I apologized to her for it, and thanked her for the grace she granted me as I was learning how to be a grown-up. She talked to me about what happened with Oakley, and told me that she had held on to the bad until she realized that she was actively preventing herself from enjoying life. She encouraged me to forgive Oakley. My chest puffed with pride as I told her that I didn't need to do so. She laughed at my inability to acknowledge my own pain and ended our conversation with one word, forgiveness. Eventually I did just that, and I realized that Oakley had done me a huge favor. It took months of work, but I granted myself grace as well as the space and time necessary to heal. But I had a feeling that if I didn't confront Oakley, this Christmas would undo all of that healing.

"Steve, I'll see y'all tonight for dinner right?" I asked attempting to wrap up our conversation so I could finish grading the last shreds of work. The last thing I wanted to do was take it home with me. He asked if I was ready to be set up on a blind date yet. "You surely didn't invite an unsuspecting woman to dinner did you?" Once he assured me that he had not, I told him that I'd let him know when I was ready.

I wrapped my conversation with Steve,

watched the last of the buses pull off and hid in my classroom grading my students' holiday themed short stories for the next hour or so. The last one I had been really eager to read. This was my writer. He could pull together a string of words that pulled you in and transported you to another location entirely. His short story was the length of a novella and good enough to be published. I wrote the most encouraging thing I could on his work in hopes of letting him know that, man to man, he was a talented writer and that it was cool to be himself. Having finished grading for the week, I closed up my classroom - lights turned off, chairs pushed in, trash taken out - for the weekend, and headed out to my car.

The near-winter winds in Kansas City were angry and quick to let you know they were present. I heard them, felt them smack me on the face, and realized that I'd left my scarf in the classroom. At that point I was already committed to the cold-weather shuffle and was more than halfway to my car, which would be a great refuge from the wind. I hopped in my car and headed to my house. What a day, what a week, but I felt lucky to be doing the work that I knew would make a difference, no matter how tiring it was.

I had just enough time to work out and get cleaned up before heading to Steve's house, which was only a 10 minute drive across town.

I decided to get pseudo dressed up just in case he had invited another person to eat dinner with us. I could never be too sure when it came to him feeling like I was ready to be set up, whether I was actually prepared or not. He and Sabrina had both been threatening to set me up for the last few months. So a nice shirt vs. a t-shirt was the way to go. Better safe than sorry I suppose.

Jax opened the door for me when I arrived, "Hi Mr. Charlie!"

"Hey Jax! Did you stop all that flipping business yet?"

He giggled and told me that he was working on perfecting a dance move that his "friend" Lola would love. I glanced in Sabrina's direction and watched as she shook her head and pointed knowingly at Steve, "That's YOUR child, Steve."

Grinning from ear to ear, Steve shook his head at the thought of passing along the showboating trait. The world was barely ready for it when Steve was doing it. There's no way they'd be ready for Jax.

"Can I show you the dance, Mr. Charlie?" Jax asked hopping around the room.

"MAYBE after dinner, Jax." He hopped more vigorously. "MAYBE! Maybe!" I added, urging him to calm down with my words.

I knew it would only buy me a few moments because if there's one thing that I've learned about children, it's that they will forget the information that you just taught them 5 minutes ago, but if you hint at the possibility of something fun, they'll remember that for months to come - remember that time you said we might get some extra recess time if we were all good in our music class? When are we going to get that?

Dinner was great. We chatted about the work that Steve and Sabrina are doing, then about how this school year is going compared to last year - my first in the classroom full-time. What I knew for certain, is that my life was growing in a positive direction and I told them such. They expressed their happiness which was always followed by a question that I was prepared for Sabrina to ask, but it came from Jax instead tonight.

"So when are you going to bring someone to dinner with you, Mr. Charlie?" I almost spit, okay, I did spit my drink back in my cup.

"Jax!" Sabrina attempted to redirect his question, but it was far too late.

"I promise I won't bring anybody around you unless I'm 100% sure we're going to get married," I said, hoping to buy myself a load of time.

"Got it!" he said, content in the answer I had provided to him. "Mr. Charlie, it's after dinner!" he said, springing from the table.

"It is," I said, looking at his Dad for some help in finding another activity other than...

It was too late. He had already mistimed his flip and was laying on the floor screaming in agony. My stomach was in knots. I could see his left arm and it was bent in a place where it was supposed to be as straight as a rod. His mom grabbed him from the floor and rushed to their car in the garage. I grabbed my coat and followed, knowing I'd need to move my car before they could go anywhere. Steve followed behind me to close the house. We all knew they were headed to the Emergency Room, and nobody had to say a word.

I backed out of the driveway then followed them to Hope Gardens in a hurry. I parked my car and ran in to see if I could find them, noticing Steve's illegally parked car on the way. They had just been seated in something called the Family Room when I got there, and I heard them paging a doctor to their location. I offered to move Steve's car to a legal parking spot for them so they could focus all of their energy on Jax. Steve handed me the keys, I patted Jax on the head and reassured him that everything would get better soon. He nodded, tears staining his face. "Chin up," I told him and dashed off to move their car.

By the time I moved their car and returned to the Family Room, Steve and Jax were gone. So I handed the keys to Sabrina and sat with her until she received word about the game plan to fix Jax's arm. "How you doing mom?" I asked her.

"I don't even know when he started doing all of this flip business. I feel like I failed him."

"No. You didn't fail him. Those are Steve's genes, remember?" I said trying to lighten the mood.

"Oh trust me, I remember him flipping over that wall. I thought he had hurt himself, so I went to check on him. The two of you were the worst."

"I know."

"You knew I thought he had busted his head open and you acted like there was an emergency."

"I remember."

"I should've walked away then."

"Nah, you couldn't walk away. He needed you so he could stop doing all that stupid stuff."

"I guess."

"We both needed you to help straighten us up."

"Y'all were a mess."

"I still am."

"We're all a work in progress," she said. "Don't be so hard on yourself."

I looked at her and shook my head. "Jax is as well, mom. Don't beat yourself up over this one. Now when he comes home with a face tattoo, I'm pointing fingers."

"That will still be his daddy's genes," she said chuckling through her tears.

About the same time as she received a text from Steve that they were able to reset Jax's arm, a social worker stepped in to ask her about the accident. Sabrina shared what happened and the social worked asked if there was anyone else present. I spoke up and shared my version of the story, which began when I saw Jax flip off the bench at school and called his father to let him know what I had seen.

Sabrina's face told the full tale of exactly what she was feeling internally. I told her that I was going to head out so she could be with her family and she hugged me, thanked me for being present, and apologized for this unexpected trip to the hospital. I served her words right back to her.

"Don't be so hard on yourself sis. He's going to heal, grow, and hopefully learn that flipping to impress a girl isn't as spectacular as his dad made it out to be. Hug Steve and Jax for me."

And with that I was off. I wasn't quite ready to head home yet, but I didn't know what I wanted to do. Holiday cheer was everywhere and I was hoping to avoid as much of that as possible. The best place I knew to get that was to head back to the place where I met Oakley, the Fresh Grind coffeehouse.

I headed to the parking garage to get my car and drove around for a bit first, building up the nerve to completely move on from Oakley. I realized as I drove though, that it wasn't her I was stalling for, it was me. I remembered my phone call with Cheryl and her urging me to forgive and open myself up to something greater. That was the real fear. All I could see was someone who might hurt me again the way I had allowed myself to be hurt before. But Cheryl promised there would be something greater, which I wasn't focusing on. Instead, I was only looking at the possibility of all of the bad things that might happen. I couldn't get anywhere thinking about that. I found the closest parking spot to the Fresh Grind and threw the car into Park like a boss. Still missing my scarf, I zipped my coat as far as it would go then stepped out into my future.

She was working tonight, Oakley was, and I was thinking about what I would say to her when I saw her. Before I could do so, I found myself falling into the person who was standing in front of me and catching the culprit that bumped me, before she broke something like Jax. I'd seen enough of that for one day but I hadn't expected what was next.

She was beautiful. I was so caught off guard that I couldn't find the right words but I was glad that I chose the dress shirt over the t-shirt.

She attempted to apologize to me. I called her fine and made her so uncomfortable that she wouldn't look at me. I was bumbling through this one. What was wrong with me? My brain was moving a mile a minute but not all of the words were making it to my mouth. I attempted to give myself a pep talk, "*I. am. not. this. guy. Get it together, Charlie!*"

"...you're okay," I said. She looked at me like she felt sorry for me and thanked me with hesitance in her voice. I was about to screw this one up and I never saw it coming.

I was at a loss for words and had been basking in her presence. Without realizing how much time had passed, I laughed at my good fortune. We literally stumbled into each other, right after I vowed to be open to something greater. What if she was that something greater?

I apologized for making things awkward and offered to buy her apple cider, with sugarplums. I really thought I was the only one who added that spiced goodness to their cider. Who was this woman? She flat refused and offered to buy my drink. When I told her it was the same as hers, I don't think she believed me to be genuine. Before I knew it the barista was asking for our order and mystery woman was attempting to separate hers from mine. I interjected, and offered our order, hoping it didn't look to much like an over-assuming jerk move. She glanced at me, but it didn't seem to be a glare. Maybe I would be okay after all. She asked for them to add cinnamon extract to one of them, which sounded great.

"Both of them," I added.

We moved towards the cash register and I had completely forgotten that I was in the same location where I met...

"Hey Charlie!" That voice. It was Oakley. She made an assumption that I was getting both ciders and the mystery woman looked noticeably uncomfortable. Confronting Oakley was easier than I thought it was going to be, but I had help from a beautiful stranger.

I told Oakley that one cider was mine and the other belonged to, I paused realizing that I hadn't yet asked her name. This had to set a record for the longest fumble ever. I was blowing it. I didn't have to pay for the drinks thanks to Oakley, oddly enough. I'm not sure why she offered to pay for them. There had to be some ulterior motive. No way was she just being nice.

Mystery woman seemed like she was in a hurry and as much as I wanted her to stay, I knew that I couldn't stand in her way. I had slipped behind her so we wouldn't awkwardly bump into each other again, and I could see that she was looking for me. I cleared my throat which startled her. I thought I was about to catch a hot cider bath and closed one eye in anticipation of being drenched with the steaming drink. Instead she turned slowly, raising her drink to thank me.

I raised mine in return and thanked her for bumping into me, attempting to draw out our conversation so she wouldn't leave. I could tell it was coming. She was already leaning towards the door.

"So listen, I'd love to learn more about the person who created the first coffee chain... reaction," I joked. It garnered a smile that she quickly suppressed. She told me she was running in to quickly grab a drink before heading home from a long shift. There was so much more that I wanted to know, but I knew I had to be respectful. The more I pushed, the closer she got to the door. I thanked her for bumping into me. She thanked me for the cider. I tried to ask her name without being too forward. The ball was finally out of my hands. The fumble was complete. But she offered a lifeline, "Great, hope to bump into you here again!" and just like the snap of the fingers she was gone. I didn't want to stay there for too long, but I also didn't want her to think I was chasing her down by leaving behind her. I fumbled around with the stirring sticks, napkins, and spoons for a while before leaving. I could feel Oakley's eyes on me the whole time. I tipped my cup in her direction to thank her for the ciders for me and the mystery woman and hopped in my car to head home.

Before I could get away from the Fresh Grind, my phone rang. It was Steve, giving me an update on Jax and thanking me for being there for his family when they needed it.

"No problem. So hey man," I paused.

"Wait, where are you Charlie?" Steve asked me.

"I'm leaving the Fresh Grind," I hesitated, knowing that he'd call me out on being in the same place as Oakley.

"Did you go see Oakley?" he asked, his voice raising an octave or two as he spoke.

"I did, and I fell."

"You what? Man, that woman, you remember..."

"No no. I literally fell. I was bumped into another customer which set off a chain reaction and the woman who bumped into me was, whoa."

"Not whoa. What's her name? What does she do? Tell me about her? Wait, was Oakley there?"

"I don't know her name or what she does. I only know she was in there to order an apple cider with a spoonful of sugarplums."

"You are THE ONLY person I know who orders that."

"I know. But I'm not alone. She offered to pay for my drink even though I tried to pay for hers. Turns out Oakley ended up buying the drinks for us."

"So she was there."

"She was, but she was a non-issue. I forgot she was there. I focused solely on trying to get to know this woman in the 5 minutes that I had with her."

"So you didn't get her name?"

"I got nothing, except a free drink from Oakley."

"Bro." His single word held so much meaning embedded within it.

"I know man, I have to do better."

"Nope. Not what I was going to say. Remember when I flipped for Sabrina?"

"Yeah. That was some foolishness."

"Ha ha. I would stumble over my words every time I saw her. I couldn't get a word out edgewise. The only thing I could do was run up a wall and flip and I darn near busted my head doing so. But she thought I was hurt and came running over to see if I needed help."

"Yeah."

"You only fumble when..."

"No. We're not doing that."

"Not doing what?"

"I don't know this woman's name. I don't know what she does. Oakley was acting a fool in there too."

"Who cares about Oakley?! We're talking about this mystery woman."

"I'll probably never see her again. You know

Kansas City," I reassured him.

"I do know Kansas City," Steve assured me. "It's super small."

"Nah, man. I need to let her go. Plus, I'm assuming she's single. She had on gloves, I couldn't see if she was married. I'm tripping."

"Well give it a day or two and see if she pops up again before you just write her off."

"Yeah, okay," I said, pretending to be disinterested all of a sudden.

"Well, while you're waiting it out, I did notice that there wasn't a ring on the finger of the doctor who took care of Jax."

"No way man. You're not setting me up on a date with someone you don't even know."

"I mean she's..."

"No." I had just pulled up in front of my house and needed to run inside. So I started to curtail the phone call.

"Okay, man. If you change your mind about the doctor, let me know. We're here until tomorrow morning and I can put in a good word about how you saved us yesterday."

I side-stepped any commitment to being set up on a blind date and instead sat down to enjoy my cider and wind down for the day. I fell asleep wondering about all the what-ifs. This woman had invaded my thoughts and I didn't know a single thing about her. Give it a day or two, the last thought I remember saying to myself, replaying Steve's words in my mind.

Fast forward to a beautifully chilly Saturday morning that I spent relaxing in the best possible way - cleaning up after the mess I had left for myself throughout the rest of the week. By the time I finished, I realized that I hadn't gone to the grocery store. My stomach grumbled the groans of a hundred angry beetles, and I needed to grab some lunch. There was a little cafe I had been wanting to try, so I got cleaned up, grabbed my keys, and headed out for The Fresh Pantry, which was right across the street from the Fresh Grind. I was approaching the cafe from across the street when I saw a very familiar face.

Maybe Steve was right, give it a couple of days he said. It hadn't even been 24 hours and there was the mystery woman, in the same cafe that I was about to eat lunch in. I could not believe my good fortune. Maybe I could sit down with her to find out more about who she is. I pulled out my phone, about to dial Steve's number so I could tell him what was about to go down, but before I could dial, a man sat down across from her in the same booth. She smiled at him, appearing to be happy to see his face. It felt like the wind had been knocked out of me...again. But how? I didn't know anything about this woman, but I had the answer to the biggest piece of the puzzle. She was not single. Before I could call Steve, my phone rang. It was him, letting me know that they were on their way home.

Disappointment coursed all through my veins, as I did an about-face and walked into the Fresh Grind, telling him about the mystery woman.

"Mmm hmmm," he said, then asked again about whether or not I wanted to be set up on a blind date with the doctor.

Knowing that the mystery woman was out of the question, I said yes, before I could stop the words from coming out of my mouth. "Done."

I had no clue why I walked into the coffeehouse. There was no way that I had any business going back into the place where Oakley worked. I knew she'd think it was a sign of interest, but I was hungry, they had sandwiches, and that was the closest place for me to escape before mystery woman had the chance to see me.

Never mind, Saturday. I thought we were going to be cool.

Chapter 3
Oakley

Charlie just bounced back into the coffeehouse. I knew when I saw him yesterday that it wouldn't take long for him to return. He never could spend that much time away from me when we were "a thing." I have to say, his presence still brings a tingle to my spine and so many memories - good and bad.

I'll always remember the first time he walked into the Fresh Grind with his friends and their baby child human. I'm not at all comfortable around other people's children, but they had swooped in off the street to warm up, and well, Charlie...Charlie was so fine I placed my hands over my heart and proceeded to swoon over the baby. I could tell that he had wealth on his side, Charlie, not his friend - he looked exhausted by that tiny attention suck, as did his wife. But I didn't stay focused on them for too long. I was too drawn to Charlie. His dark heather gray wool coat, maroon and orange plaid paperboy hat, and matching cashmere scarf gave away his affluence, and the lamb skin leather gloves cleared up any doubt. When I saw him, my world as it was stopped. I knew that he could be my path out of the coffee house. I mean I even had visions of marrying him and becoming a Real Housewife of Kansas City. All glamour and no work. I did everything within my power to become a person he couldn't live without.

In all honesty, Charlie came into my life at a time where I was picking up the pieces after being left by the jerk that was my ex-fiance. That dolt took everything from me including things I hadn't even realized I had given away. I had a job as an actuary, working for one of the largest insurance companies here in Kansas City. He and I had dated since college. It was by all descriptions a whirlwind romance. We met during our sophomore year at a mixer in the residence halls. I was there with my roommate, Jen, and she kept motioning to this strange guy in a bucket hat.

"What are you doing?" I asked in exasperation.

Giggling an iron-willed call of submission in my direction, she waved at him once more, further solidifying my desire to request another roommate.

"He's coming this way, girl! Get your stuff together," Jen strained through her toothy grin.

"I'm done with you. Who is that? I can't even see his face past that bucket on his head!" I sighed.

"Excuse me ladies. I couldn't help but notice the two of you from across..."

"Stop it." There was no way I was letting him finish that statement.

"I'm sorry?" he asked, raising one eyebrow and flashing a crooked smile.

"You have the nerve to come over here and act like you and Jen weren't signing to each other all night. I'm not a fool. Don't try to run game on me," I insisted, cracking a smile at the two of them.

He laughed with a rumble so deep I thought I could feel it in the pit of my stomach. Turns out, those were the butterflies that always seemed to take flight after he flashed that crooked smile of his. I turned away from him, hoping to hide the flushed look on my own face. I had a sneaking suspicion that this was going to be one of those relationships that would define a pivotal moment for me. I was right.

"Jenson Norris," he said, extending a hand to shake mine. It was warm and firm, yet his touch was soft. So was my heart and we were pretty much inseparable after that.

Football games, watch parties, study sessions, breakfast, lunch and dinner in The Caf, movie nights, casino night, parties in the Union, house parties, Black Student Union meetings, you name it, we were there together. Jenson was my safe place, my home away from home, the first person I would call when I passed a test or struggled with a term paper and he did the same with me.

We spent our Christmases with my family and our New Year's Eves with his. His sister became my sister, and my younger brother looked up to him like he was the best man in the world, often calling him to talk about the game or how to approach a girl he liked at school. It all seemed so natural and easy. We talked often about the type of jobs we would have once we graduated, the type of city or town we would live in, how big our first, second, and third house were going to be, our future children, Kerry and Corbyn, and where we were going to retire for both the warm and cold months. I'd had a bit of anxiety leading up to the end of my senior year because after 3 years of routine, relative safety and contentment, things were going to change. They had to.

The day of our graduation he was more quiet than I've ever seen him. His ceremony was first so our families (his and mine) all went to the coliseum at 8:00 in the morning to cheer as he walked across the stage. We popped over to our favorite hamburger joint, a hidden treasure from the main row of eateries in this college town, for a quick lunch afterward. He was still quiet. The weeks leading up to commencement he had stopped talking about the future. I didn't know what to make of it. All I could do was reassure him where I stood with respect to our relationship, but it didn't feel like it made a difference to him. So I didn't bring it up when we were at lunch. We just ate and smiled awkwardly at each other, then returned to the coliseum at 2:00 for my ceremony.

I stood with the other graduates in my college and nervously got in line to shake hands with the deans and grab the degree I was merited. The closer I got to the front, the more nostalgic I became. Every step sent me deeper into a spiral of memories until my eyes had glazed over with thoughts of the good and bad moments that I was about to leave behind for true adulthood. Tears began to build in my eyes and I thought about venturing into that world without Jenson.

I remember hearing them announce my name, "Oakley Powell, Bachelor's of Science Degree, Accounting." I remember walking confidently across the stage in what felt like slow motion; nodding at the department head, shaking hands with the Dean of the College of Business, hearing my family and Jenson's shouting congratulations, spotting them in the crowd, smiling and waving at them, pausing for a photo, then off the stage. Those ten seconds felt like ten minutes. I can still feel every blink, every inhale, every exhale, the motion as I ambled down every step in my heels, the tug at my heartstrings when I realized that Jenson wasn't sitting with our families, the warmth of the tear that fell from my left eye and coursed its way to the floor, the walk back towards my seat knowing that we were done, the joy I felt in seeing his face as the graduate in front of me turned towards our row, the smile that creased my face from ear to ear as I got closer to him, the moment my heart skipped a beat as he dropped down to one knee and extended a hand to me, the sound of the collective "woo" of the graduates immediately beside us as he knelt down, the moment he held my hand while down on bended knee. At that moment, time stood still and though I know there were graduates behind me, I don't remember them passing me at all. I just remember his face, so serious and full of anxiety.

"You and me, Oakley," he paused, choking down the emotions causing a lump in his throat. "That's all I've known for the past three years. That's all I've felt each day we're together. That's all I want in the future. You and me, raising Kerry and Corbyn, retiring and spoiling our grandchildren. But I can only have that if you want it too. We can only have that if we work together. Will you take this adventure with me?"

I cried like my dog had died. Suddenly the thoughts I had about everything coming to a close had vanished. They had been replaced with the promise of the future we had crafted together.

"Oakley, will you marry me?"

I couldn't get any words out, but I looked him in the eyes and nodded, sniffling away any potential disaster created by a runny nose.

"I need to hear the word, Oak," he said with that crooked smile.

"Yes, Jenson, YES!" I shouted. The graduates

beside us cheered, so too did the crowd to our left after Jenson removed the ring from its black velvet box and slowly slid it over my knuckle and onto its new home on my finger.

I was ready to face the world with him. My confidence had been restored.

Jenson had received a job offer in Kansas City that provided enough for him to take care of both of us while I found work. He didn't have to carry me for too long though. I found a job within two weeks of graduation which meant I only had a week between our move and when I started work myself. Since we were now planning a wedding, we shared a place together and also opened a joint bank account. That all made sense at the time, but in hind sight that was probably the worst thing I could have done.

None of what happened next was anticipated. In fact, things had felt the same as they did in college. We'd talk about each other's day, but this time instead of being centered on our classes, discussion was about what we were learning on the job. Speaking of which, mine was going exceedingly well. Just four short months on the job and I was receiving high praise from my supervisors. They were connecting me to people who would be willing to serve as my mentor, then before I knew it, the bottom fell out.

I had gone out to lunch with a few co-workers for Taco Tuesday and tried to use my debit card to pay (only for my meal mind you) but it was declined. I had them try once more, and again it was declined. Thankfully, I had a co-worker spot me a lunch until I could figure out what was going on with the bank. As we drove back to work I called Jenson to give him a heads up, but he didn't answer the phone. While it wasn't uncommon for him to answer his phone during a workday, that non-answer was actually the start of my downfall. I left him a voicemail and finished the rest of the work day. When I got home I received my third surprise for the day.

As it turns out, for several months Jenson had failed to pay the rent on the house we were renting and I came home to an eviction notice posted on the front door, while my clothes and other belongings were in boxes on the front yard. Tears welled up in my eyes as I tried to figure out what was going on. I called Jenson again, and this time the phone went directly to voicemail. I called my Dad to get his help on what to do and he encouraged me to visit Jenson's job to connect with him and figure out what on earth was going on. I hopped back in my car and hustled across town to his office, where I discovered my fourth surprise for the day. One was tough enough to manage. Two of them were stressful to say the least. Three was about all that I thought I could take, and then that theory would be pushed to its limits. When I arrived at the office I was greeted by the front desk attendant who remembered me to be Jenson's fiancée. His eyebrows turned in towards each other like they were about to give each other a high five. That mystified expression let me know that something was off. I braced for impact as he opened his mouth to speak.

"So, are you applying for Jenson's position or...," he paused waiting for some sort of confirmation.

"Jenson's position?" Now it was time for my eyebrows to fist bump in solidarity.

"Oh, sorry honey. I assumed he told you about what happened."

I slow blinked to catch my breath before my knees bucked and I passed out. In chatting with the attendant I was informed that Jenson had been fired from his job 3 months to the day that I showed up.

I booked it over to the bank before they closed and found surprise number five. Jenson had cleaned out our bank account. I sat sobbing in the guest chair in the office of the branch manager and asked what I was able to do.

"I wish I had better news for you honey," she started. "With him listed as the head of household on your account there isn't anything that he needs your permission for. The opposite though is true for you."

"Can I stop my checks from being deposited into the account?" I asked, hoping for some reassurance that they could redirect them into a different account.

"Unfortunately we are unable to do that unless the two of you sign a specific form together to do so."

I was outdone and so very confused. I thanked her for her time and stood up, realizing in that moment that I was homeless and penniless until my next paycheck hit, which would be another 15 days. I called Jenson's mom. No answer. I called his Dad. No answer. I called his Sister, my sister for the last 3 years. Nothing. I searched for them online and couldn't find any of them. I had been blocked. What was going on?

I called my Dad with an update and will never forget the words he said to me in that call, "I know you're thinking the worst in this, be patient until you see what happened."

I returned to work, the only place I knew

of where I could stay in peace. When I arrived, Jerry at our front desk made a phone call with a serious look on his face - one that said I was guilty of something.

"She's here. Yes, I'll hold her."

This had to be a dream. What was going on?

"Jerry?" I quivered out through shallow breaths.

"Where's your badge Ms. Powell?"

"Jerry? What's going on?"

Before I could finish my sentence the door to the lobby swung open with a force so hard it hit the wall. Out stepped my supervisor who asked me to sit down.

"We had high hopes for you Oakley. Unfortunately we cannot take the risk to continue your employment with our company."

"What risks?" I asked, just as confused as I was when my debit card didn't work at lunch.

"We received a note from your fiance requesting the immediate creation of a life insurance policy on you so that he could take out a loan," she sighed then continued, "I don't want to tell you how bad that looks, but that you would choose a partner like this also speaks to your level of discernment."

"He did, what?" Another bombshell. It was during this conversation that I felt my entire soul leave my body.

"Unfortunately in a job where your discernment has an immediate impact on our bottom line, we're going to have to let you go. Security is bringing down a box of your personal belongings. I will need your badge though."

I could feel the heat from my anger seething through the skin on my face. I was beyond hot, and embarrassed, and because I was no longer tied to my soul, my heart went to a really petty place and just hung out there for a spell. I had been an empty shell ever since, hopping from person to person, and job to job in an attempt to fill my life up with meaning again.

Then all of the sudden there he was, this handsome face, and someone who from the looks of it knew how to manage money. My second chance at reclaiming the old Oakley, the one who cared about people and making a difference in the world. The one who knew how to love.

I cooed over that tiny baby child human as though I cared, when in reality it stung to see two people fatigued and in love in a way that I had always envisioned my life with Jenson. I wanted what they had, and here was Charlie, a definite maybe in the love arena.

We weren't very busy that night so I had the opportunity to visit their table to see if they needed anything else. Steve, obviously playing wingman, asked if I had any plans to visit some of the sights and sounds of Christmas in Kansas City.

I responded to his wife, "I only have a couple of days off during the week and those hours tend to vary because I'm in the service industry."

Charlie offered to take me around the town so I could enjoy the Christmas season.

"Oh yeah? What would we do?" I asked him.

"A trip to the theater to see A Christmas Carol or The Nutcracker, a visit to one of the local college's holiday music festivals, a trip to the Plaza and a carriage ride around the town, a visit to see the Mayor's Christmas tree, sit on Santa's lap. The usual, you know?"

"Let's put one of those on the calendar." I

said with a chuckle and a wink in his direction before returning to the counter.

Charlie and Steve laughed, but Sabrina, she made sure to stop by the counter on their way out to get my phone number for Charlie.

I received a call from him that night to, "verify the accuracy of this phone number." We ended up chatting on the phone for hours and before I knew it, it was almost time for me to rise and start the day again - except I hadn't gone to bed yet. Through our phone call I discovered that Charlie was living in Chicago, so we planned to meet again before he returned there for the week.

That date was one of my favorites. We didn't do anything except get coffee and people watch, but I didn't feel like I needed to put on a performance around him. It was like we had known each other for years and were just catching up on old times. He left that evening and we spoke on the phone every night that week. He made plans to return the following weekend so we could have our Kansas City Christmas date, and he made good on that promise.

We did everything that he told me he'd do and I fell hard at the idea of loving this man. We spoke on Christmas Day and he snuck into

Kansas City to be my New Years's Eve date. It was a whirlwind romance and I felt like a princess being courted by a prince. We had gotten all dolled up to attend a fancy New Year's Eve Ball. We laughed and danced the night away like a couple who was secure in their relationship, and then the countdown to the new year had begun. We twirled around the dance floor with one minute left before the year changed when I asked him,

"What's your New Year's Resolution?"

He told me about his desire to become a teacher and I told him about the program that my friend had encouraged me to apply for. His gaze shifted from a look of admiration to one of adoration. His face opened up towards mine and he leaned in ever so slightly to softly whisper the countdown in my ear.

"10." My heart began to flutter.
"9." My breathing increased ten-fold.
"8." He used the hand resting on the small of my back to gently pull me in closer.
"7." My knees broke.
"6." I rested my hand on his chest to steady my balance.
"5." I closed my eyes for just a moment to take it all in, knowing that the new year was about to bring something much different

than I had experienced in a long time.
"4." I inhaled slowly, tilted my head back and opened my eyes to meet his.
"3." He unknowingly smiled at me, as though he had a plan for us.
"2." He used his other hand to squeeze the one I had placed on his chest.
"1." I felt his heart rate increase as he dipped his chin towards his chest and leaned in for a kiss.

Our noses grazed each others and just before our lips met his phone rang. He placed his forehead on mine and we took a heartbeat to take in the moment before he spoke softly.

"It's my mom. She always calls me at midnight."

"Happy New Year," I whispered, still hoping to regain the strength in my legs.

He kissed my forehead before answering the phone, still swaying the night away, "Happy New Year, Mom!"

I was open to love in ten seconds flat. That must have been some kind of record.

Throughout the course of the next few months, Charlie applied for and was accepted into the Teaching Fellows program, which brought him to Kansas City halfway into the new year. Things were going well. Almost too well, which is what raised a flag that something was about to happen. The feeling in the pit of my stomach that I tried to shake was the second inkling that something was coming.

As Charlie made lifestyle adjustments to accommodate his salary as a Teacher, we ate in more often than we ate out. The number of Galas we attended were more infrequent. He began the academic year and his level of stress was through the roof. I didn't know how to help him with the stress, but I wanted to. Then it happened, I received an email from the man who disappeared without a trace and with all of my money.

It read:

> Oak,
>
> I know I'm the last person you probably expected to hear from. I can explain, but we need to talk about it in person. Let me know when you're free to talk and if you have the same phone number.
>
> I'm sorry,
> Jenson

An email, from Jenson. Charlie and I had talked about what happened in my last relationship. He knew I was engaged. He knew that Jenson disappeared without a trace or so much as a word. We both thought that I had received closure, but the way I felt after this email says I didn't. I wanted an answer. I deserved an answer. I couldn't bring myself to tell Charlie about this. I just wanted to confront Jenson, find out what happened, get it over with and move on.

I replied:

> Jenson. My phone number is the same. Call me at 8:00pm tonight to get an address of where we can meet. It will be a public place so I am not tempted to seek revenge.
>
> Oakley

Before I could close my email app, I received a simple reply.

"Will do."

I timed my work break for 7:58 so I could have enough time to find a quiet spot to listen. My phone rang right at 8 o'clock. I didn't recognize the phone number, but I knew the only person who would be calling at this time was Jenson.

"Yes?" I answered firmly.

"Oak. I'm sorry." It sounded like he truly was, but I had placed a wall around my heart when it came to Jenson.

"Meet me at The Fresh Grind Coffeehouse anytime between now and 10:00pm. I'm at work."

"Tonight?"

"Yep. Tonight or not at all." I hung up.

I went back to work behind the counter. That call took all of 2 minutes. Twenty minutes later the door to the coffeehouse opened up and I knew it was him. His eyes scanned the entirety of the coffeehouse in search of me. I motioned for him to get in line to place an order.

"Could I have a large coffee? Black."

The barista prepared his coffee and Jenson paid at the register, looking me dead in my eyes without saying a word, only a nod and a $10 tip. I motioned with my head towards a booth in the back of the coffeehouse. The rage that I imagined I would feel was non existent. Instead I was filled with curiosity.

He sat in the back, nursing his coffee and every so often glancing my way. Once things slowed down, I meandered my way back to his booth and sat down. "Talk."

"You look good, Oak."

"Not that. You don't get to..."

"I'm sorry. I wish I could have. Pause. I wish I would have told you what was going on with me before I left."

I looked at him stone-faced, guarding my heart.

He shared everything that happened in his words. He was blackmailed by someone who got him fired and then asked for more money than we had available. He thought he would be able to get a new job, but found out that his name had been blackballed in his industry. He told me that he had instructed his family not to answer any calls from me, so that he would have time to fix things. I listened and believed him. That one-time visit to explain what happened turned into regular drop-ins to see how I was doing. Before I knew it we had reconnected and things began to escalate. You know how you exercise and lose weight, then when you stop exercising your weight comes back ten-fold in far less time than it took for you to lose the weight to begin with? It was like that. It all happened so fast that I didn't have time to tell Charlie about it, at least that's what I told myself.

I fell into a pattern where I would tell myself that I'd talk to Charlie that night, then that night we would talk about the future and he would look at me with the same gaze from New Year's Eve. Then I couldn't bring myself to hurt him. About a week before Christmas, Jenson picked me up on my lunch break and surprised me with a trip to a jeweler. We were "just looking" at rings when he asked the jeweler to size the one that I wanted. As the jeweler came in from the back, in walked Charlie. I was still beaming from the shock of Jenson's surprise when I turned and saw his face.

"Mr. Hughes! I have your ring in the back. Just let me finish sizing this couple's ring really quickly and I'll grab it for you," the jeweler said to Charlie before turning to Jenson and I to chat about the selection waiting in the back. "This guy must REALLY love his woman! Three carats, this guy!"

"Congratulations, my man!" Jenson said,

genuine excitement flowing from his lips. I squeezed him to stop him, in hopes of communicating to him that this was Charlie, my Charlie. His face was devoid of emotion. It looked like someone had ripped his soul from his body, just as had been done to me. Unwittingly I had just put him through the same thing as I felt because I couldn't be honest with him when I received the first email.

He stormed out of the jewelry shop before I could say anything. I tried to follow him, but I still had the freshly resized ring on my finger. I tugged and tugged, but it had cooled around my finger and I couldn't get it off quickly enough. By the time I could, Charlie was gone, out of my life for good. I tried to call him. I sent emails that bounced back to my account. I sent unreturned texts. I hoped he would come see me at work so I could explain myself, especially since it wouldn't be a good idea for me to show up at his school. I had become the very person I loathed, just a few months before. I owed Charlie an explanation, but most of all I owed him some space. The space to be hurt, to be angry, to hate me, to miss me, to want an answer.

I owed him all of that, no matter how much time it took, and no matter how much I wanted to explain it now. So I gave Charlie time and space, and he didn't return.

I never fully believed Jenson, I only wanted to feel like I was still special to him. So the thing that broke up Charlie and I, ended up being a flash in the continuum of time and not even worth the energy I gave it in the first place.

I had a hole in my soul again, but this time, I had done it to myself.

For about a year I wondered if I would ever have the chance to speak to him again. Then in he walked yesterday. He greeted me with a smile and acted like he was with some other woman who he had just met, but I knew better. She left without even giving him her name, which told me that my presence wouldn't disrupt a relationship that he might have been in, because there's no way he would flirt with a woman like that if he were in a relationship with someone else. He didn't have that kind of bone in his body. Well, maybe he didn't. There was a time that people would have said that about me. I hoped that my decisions didn't change him in that way. It was a bad space to reside.

After SHE left, he fidgeted with the napkins and stirring sticks for a while before turning towards me and lifting his cup in my direction in thanks. I smiled. He hadn't completely ignored me which was a good sign. I thought about our relationship all night; how we had met, when we had met, the moment he saw me differently than just someone he was dating that New Year's Eve, how many opportunities I had to do things differently. I messed that up. I wasn't ready, even though I thought I could get there. I only hoped that he would find his way back into the coffeeshop again so I could apologize to him.

Little did I know that would happen sooner than I would know. So here he was, bounding back into the store again at lunch time. Here we were face to face. I knew when he tipped his cup at me that he'd be back. I saw it in his eyes, that he wasn't ready to walk away from me yet.

"Charlie!"

"Oakley." *So cold and formal.*

He kept looking over his shoulder so I asked the obvious questions, too unnerved to ask anything deeper, "Are you okay? Are you running from something?"

"I'm okay, do you still have the chicken salad sandwich here?" He was strictly business, but why was he here?

"We do, can I get you some chips with that?" I asked, keeping it formal myself.

“Uh yeah, some Kettle Cooked.”

“Jalapeño?”

“Yep,” he raised one eyebrow towards me like he was surprised that I remembered. I remembered far more than he knew.

“We do,” I said. “It’s on the house. We’ll bring it out to you in a moment.”

“I insist on paying for my food Oakley. I know this is your coffee shop and all, but you don’t have to comp me.”

“Your money’s no good here, Charlie. Really.”

He nodded and found his way to an open booth with a street view where he both gazed out the window and appeared to hide simultaneously. I personally delivered his food to him and asked if I could sit down. He nodded without looking at me, his eyes instead fixed on the Cafe across the street. I looked in the general direction of his gaze when I saw her, the same woman from the night before. She was sitting in a booth with another man.

“Charlie, I’m really sorry about what happened with us.”

Still looking at her, he nodded.

I continued, "She's not interested in him if you're curious."

That seemed to snap him out of his trance. "How do you know that?"

"We get a look when we're interested in someone." I reached across the table and grabbed his hand. He inhaled sharply and swallowed his air.

"I always wondered what I would say to you when I saw you again, and I knew that I would see you again because we live in Kansas City."

I nodded and listened.

"It changed from month to month and now the only thing I have left to say is, 'thank you'."

Still listening.

"You have opened me up to something much greater. For a long time I hadn't forgiven you, but I've done that now and I don't need anything from you."

"No explanation needed?"

"You were with another man. What more do I need to know?" his tone held heavy irritation though he tried to fight it.

"If you ever want to know what happened, I'm open. Give her a chance though, Charlie. I could tell yesterday that she was interested in you. That guy is probably just a friend," and with that I stood up, smiled through the bittersweet feeling of knowing he might truly be gone forever, but was open to finding someone that would put him first - something I couldn't do at the time.

He nodded with a look of determination that made me wonder what was up his sleeve.

While it wasn't the outcome I was looking for, it did provide me with a bit of healing I needed. I'm open for whatever may come my way.

Chapter 4
The Check-up

Charlie:

I called Steve back after I left The Fresh Grind, to chat about the mystery woman and back out of what I'd said about the doctor.

"What is it with you and this mystery woman, man?" he asked, his voice laced with curiosity.

"I don't know what to tell you." I hesitated to say what I was thinking because it would raise a thousand questions for Steve. So instead of saying anything at all, I kept those thoughts to myself.

"Sounds like the Sabrina Effect."

He had just said exactly what I was thinking, but was hesitant to say. When they first started dating, Steve would talk to me about the dates that he and Sabrina went on and some of the conversations they had, none of which sounded like him, but all of which were done out of consideration of her feelings. I started calling them the Sabrina Effect. He talked about her non-stop, and I knew he was serious about her well before he did. He flipped up a wall to get her attention and has been voluntarily doing flips from that day forward. He could never explain it to me. All he could say was that he, "just knew."

"Ahhh. I don't know about that," I lied through my teeth, before changing the conversation to what happened with Oakley.

"So you've forgiven her?"

"I guess, yeah."

"Just like that?"

"Mm hmm."

"It's done, done?"

"Yes, I'm done. I was anxious because I knew she was in there and I hadn't spoken with her since the day before I saw her with that other man."

"Mm hmmmmm?" Steve mumbled.

"But all of the anger I had, all that I thought I was going to say to her, I didn't feel the need to say it when I saw her."

"So, how did she look?"

"I told her that, yeah."

"Charlie."

"What?"

"Man, I said 'how did she look?'"

"I know." I paused again, trying to determine whether or not it was worth a mention. "She looked good. Not gonna lie about it."

"Good."

"Good?"

"If she looked good, and you didn't feel the need to tell her where to go, then you're ready."

"For the mystery woman? I already told you that."

"No, for this good doctor I've been telling you

about."

I laughed out loud, "The good doctor. Okay, tell me more about her."

He told me all about how well she took care of Jax and made sure that we were informed and comfortable with everything before any procedures happened.

"So she has good customer service skills. What makes you so sure we'd be a good fit?"

"She's your type."

"Oakley was my type. That didn't work."

"No, Oakley was not your type. She was your pattern - unavailable women."

"So you know for certain that the good doctor is available?"

"Ask Sabrina."

"No need." Instead I asked Steve how they were going to connect the two of us together.

"So I have this case that's going to take the majority of my Friday afternoon and there's no guarantees that I'll be able to take Jax to his 1 week check-up, post new cast."

Sounded suspicious to me, but I was open to meeting this good doctor, mostly in hopes of it taking my mind off of the mystery woman. I agreed to Steve's proposal for me take Jax to his appointment from school and have Sabrina meet us there, but only if Sabrina was on board. Steve told me that it was her idea in the first place. Of course it was.

Friday came, and when he arrived at school, I reminded Jax to come to my classroom once the day was done. I reminded him again when I saw him at lunch. The students' energy level was on 10 today and I was glad that the day was drawing to a close.

"It's Friday! Forget all of this week's challenges. Relax, have fun, and..."

"DON'T SEND YOU ANY EMAILS!" they all replied with laughter.

"Stay safe so I can see you after the winter break!" I finished.

The bell sounded to close school for Winter Break and my students rushed out of the classroom faster than the speed of night. Five minutes passed, then ten minutes, and I hadn't seen Jax. I was starting to get worried that he had gotten on the bus, and was going to head to the office to find him when I heart his little feet plodding down the hallway.

Run, run, run, Skip. Hop. Hop. Run, run, run. Skip. Hop Hop.

There he was. I made sure he had all of his belongings and that I had all of mine, and we were on our way. We met Sabrina in the Family Room of Hope Gardens and they paged someone named Dr. Chris, then escorted the three of us to the Green Room.

I whispered to Sabrina as we were walking towards the room, “I thought you were setting me up with Jax's doctor.”

“Uh huh, well, we just want you to meet her,” she told me.

“They just paged, Dr. Chris to meet us in the Green Room.”

“They did.”

Jax chimed in, “Dr. Chris IS my Doctor.”

We walked in the room and had a seat, Jax on the table, Sabrina on the chair nearest him and me in the chair on the wall immediately beside the door.

Sabrina asked Jax about school and he was mid sentence when SHE sauntered in. I stood up from my seat and stuttered over my words.

"Oh. Hi. Hello. You're. Hmm. Wow."

Sabrina cut me a look that simultaneously read, "chill out bro" AND "what is happening with you?"

Dr. Chris let out a shallow breath, smiled, nodded in my direction, and kept it professional, turning her full attention to the patient, who probably could have been me given the way my heart rate had just jumped through the roof.

"Hey Jax! How's that arm treating you?"

"Good," he replied as simply as any child would when they want everything to be okay.

"Oh yeah? Any tenderness at all?" She began to test for it in different spots along the cast.

"Nope. No tenderness!" he boasted, prompting another nod and smile from Dr. Chris.

Turning her attention towards Sabrina, "Mom, good to see you again. Have you heard any complaints or noticed anything concerning?"

"None at all. Jax has taken this all in stride," Sabrina said, darting her eyes in my direction where I was still standing. *Why was I still standing?* It was too late to sit down.

Dr. Chris glanced at me from the corner of her eye, "And who else do we have supporting us today?"

"I apologize Dr. Chris, this is my husband's best friend, Mr. Hughes. He teaches at Jax's school and brought him here for his appointment today. He was also there when Jax broke his arm."

"You could say I'm invested in his healing, Dr. Chris," I said, extending a hand to greet her. She slyly smiled and shook my hand.

"It's very nice to meet you, Charlie."

Sabrina's right eyebrow raised sharply. That was her eyebrow of suspicion. She noticed something but had chosen not to say a word, opting instead to continue to cut looks in my direction. Dr. Chris continued the check-up and gave Jax two thumbs up for his progress. They wrapped the appointment and everyone eased out into the hallway. I told Sabrina that I had forgotten to ask Dr. Chris about something I had noticed at school, and I ran back to chat with her for a minute.

She was just about to leave the Green Room as I was on my way in. We almost bumped into each other - again. "Dr. Chris."

She smiled, "Charlie. Can I help you with something?"

"So I was hoping to run into you again but I had no idea it would be here." She dipped her head in embarrassment before I continued. "Sorry. No pun intended there. It's just, I'm a firm believer in fate, but I also want to be respectful of your experience here. I would love to learn more about you over lunch or dinner, or whatever fits your schedule. But I don't want to assume that you're single, or even interested."

"I would very much like that as long as you are also single," she replied. My left eyebrow raised in intrigue. Habit. I couldn't control it.

"Well it sounds like we're on the same page. I know you're on the clock and I don't want to put you in a situation where you come under any unnecessary scrutiny."

"Here's my business card, Mr. Hughes. If you notice anything abnormal with Jax's arm, give me a call. The top is my office number, the bottom is my cell."

I didn't realize I had been holding my breath the entire time until I exhaled. "Thanks, Dr. Chris. We'll be sure to keep you updated." I shook her hand once more, and both the feel of her skin and her words "I'd VERY MUCH like that," lingered in my mind with each step down the hallway.

I can't confirm it, but I feel like she watched me walk away.

Dr. Chris:

I watched him walk away.

It was only fair. Last time he got to do that as I bolted through the door of the coffee house. This time, I got to imagine that educator was mine.

He was an unexpected surprise at the end of my shift. I had just finished talking to Marlo about him last Saturday at lunch.

"So what if you bumped into him," he chided. "He caught you."

I didn't have any words. I tried. I couldn't rebut his statement. This Charlie guy had indeed caught me when he very easily could have let me fall. Then he attempted to buy my cider when he just as easily could have accepted my invitation to pay for his. Then there was the matter of Oakley, at the register, who fawned all over him.

Marlo wrote that off too, "Jealous ex. She's a non issue."

"How do you know?" I asked indignantly.

He reached across the table and held my hands. "That woman, was she pretty?"

"Without a doubt."

"Was he looking at her or looking at you?"

Again, he had rendered me silent.

"Did he look disappointed when you left?"

"He did. Like he didn't want me to go."

"So, let's recap. You accidentally bump into this Charlie. He goes out of his way to catch you as you fall. Offers to buy your drink even though you bumped into him. Then a BEAUTIFUL woman flirts with this Charlie guy, and his attention is all on you."

"Yep. Smooth criminal."

Marlo cackled, lifting my hands up from the table and sandwiching them between his before leaning in to speak. "No. I'm not going to let you talk yourself out of this one. It was right there across the street?"

I had turned my head in the direction of the Fresh Grind and saw what I thought was Charlie the mystery man, briskly walking inside.

"Chris?" he asked, snapping me back to reality.

"I think that's him."

"Let's go!" Marlo had always been the friend who was ready for action at the drop of a hat.

"No sir," I told him. "This soup is calling for me."

"Lies."

"Okay, my stomach is calling for this soup."

"Well finish up, quickly so we don't miss him," he urged. I'm pretty stubborn though, so I ate everything in my own sweet time.

We laughed and talked about everything under the sun and right as I was taking my last sip of soup, I turned back towards the coffee shop and noticed Charlie seated in a booth across from the same woman who had flirted with him the night before.

"Well, are we going to meet this Charlie or no?" Marlo asked me.

I pointed in the direction of the coffee house picture window.

"Let's just go say hi."

"No. Let's just go." Marlo knew when to push and when to drop things. Thankfully for me he chose to drop this one, but he assured me that if it was meant to be, we would be placed in the same location again. Patience, is what he told me.

Despite the way thoughts of our initial meeting seemed to sneak into my mind at the most inopportune times throughout the week, I was determined to be patient and let the universe do its thing.

Marlo checked in on me a couple of times in the week that followed, when we shared a shift together. I assured him that if the two of us reconnected, I would let him know and then I always diverted the conversation to something else. But tonight felt different, like there was a shift in the atmosphere.

"Have you put up your tree yet, Chris?"

"No, I keep picking up extra shifts and I just veg out when I get home."

"But this used to be YOUR TIME of year."

"It still is, but I just don't have the stamina to spend it the way I used to."

"Don't let the season pass you by like it did last year. Okay, boss?"

"Whatever Marlo. I'll make time for it. I always do."

An announcement rang out over the PA system, requesting my presence.

"Right on time," I joked.

"Mmm. Hmmm," Marlo said feigning irritation.

Paging Dr. Chris. Dr. Chris to the Green Room for your appointment. Paging Dr. Chris. Dr. Chris to the Green Room for your appointment.

I briskly "Doctor Walked" down the hallway to see if I could beat them into the room but had to turn around because Marlo had the clipboard that I needed. Before the check-up, I had only hoped that everything was okay with Jax's arm. Boys in elementary school can be rough so I was anticipating the worst.

When I walked through the Green Room door, I saw Jax, and his mom in the middle of a conversation. Then a familiar shaped figure abruptly stood up on the opposite side of the room. Assuming it was Jax's Dad, I turned to greet him and lost my breath. It was Charlie. He was completely out of place. *What was happening?*

When he stood up to greet me, I only nodded at him, not knowing how much information Jax and his mom were privy to. I had a hard time looking in his direction. All I could imagine was the embarrassing start to our connection. *How on earth did this happen?*

I checked in with Jax. He was fine. I was not. Still confused and a bit off-kilter, I tried my hardest not to let it show. I checked Jax's arm and did so, gingerly, mostly so I could control my own breathing. The last thing I needed was to pass out. *How did they know Charlie?*

I checked in with Jax's mom and worked hard to quiet my own inner dialogue so I could ensure that her son was okay. *How on earth did this happen?*

He was still standing. I knew I needed to acknowledge his presence, so I did so through Jax's mom. *How on earth did this happen?*

I finished the check up, left them with positive news, ushered them out of the Green Room, and sat in confusion. *How on earth did this happen? Why didn't I say anything to him?* I just let him walk away again.

I was about to head back to my office to call Marlo, but just as I crossed the threshold of the door, Charlie was on his way in, and we almost bumped into each other again. He held my elbows to ensure my safety, let me know he was interested, and then did a quick pulse check to see if I was single.

"I would very much like that as long as you are also single," I replied. His left eyebrow raised in intrigue. He looked interested, just as Marlo suggested he was.

He acknowledged that I was at work and wanted to keep it professional. He asked for my phone number without doing so directly and I wanted him to have it. I didn't want to tempt fate with phony indifference. Plus, he was holding his breath.

"Here's my business card, Mr. Hughes. If you notice anything abnormal with Jax's arm, give me a call. The top is my office number, the bottom is my cell phone."

He exhaled, thanked me for the card and shook my hand once more, I didn't want to let go, but Jax and his mom were down the hallway watching our conversation. I feel like she knew, I'm just not sure how much. Even after we let go, I could still feel the presence of his grip on my hand, and the way he looked into my soul...

How on earth did this happen?

I'm still not sure but yes, I watched. I watched as Jax ran ahead to push the elevator button. I watched as Jax's mom fought hard to keep her thoughts to herself. I watched as Charlie Hughes took the ball I had just tossed him and walked away, without so much as a swivel back in my direction, willing him with every step to call my cell phone.

Then I watched as Marlo got off the elevator and Charlie cocked his head to the side, as though he were trying to figure out why Marlo looked familiar to him.

I made eye contact with Marlo, scrunched my nose up and smiled as the elevator doors closed.

"What's with the face?" he asked me tucking his chin in towards his chest and raising his eyebrows.

I exhaled deeply, "Walk with me Marlo."

We walked back to my office where I input the information from Jax's visit and Marlo waited as patiently as he could for me to speak.

Apparently the silence was too much, "Spill it, smiley!"

"That man who got on the elevator when you were getting off."

"Yeah, the man with the woman and little boy?"

"Yep. That's Charlie."

"Mystery Man, Charlie?"

"Mystery Man, Charlie," I said definitively.

"So he has a child and a woman?" he paused. "Forget patience. Run!"

"No. He's friends with their family."

"Uh oh."

"Yep."

"So how are you going to..."

"He's a teacher at Jax's school, so I gave him my business card."

"But you don't have his phone number."

I placed one finger in the air as my cell phone started ringing. The number had a Chicago area code, but wasn't one of my contacts. I answered it, in case it was an emergency, secretly hoping it was him.

Chapter 5
The Phone Call

"This is Dr. Chris."

Marlo whispered, "It better be him!" I thrust my finger closer to his face, further emphasizing its presence.

"Hi, Dr. Chris." It was him. I nodded rapidly towards Marlo while trying to contain the smile on my face. "It's Charlie. Charlie Hughes."

"Hi, Charlie. Is everything okay with Jax?" I asked while Marlo danced in his seat across from me. I pursed my lips together, gave him "the look," and thrust my pointer finger back in his direction.

I heard Charlie audibly exhale, "It is."

"Okay good." I hoped he had more to say but there was silence. "Are you okay?" I asked him.

A faint "hm" escaped his mouth before he reeled it in. "I am. I'm sitting in my car after what felt like the longest walk I've ever taken."

Now I was silent. I closed my eyes and shook my head from side to side while Marlo asked questions, waving him out of my office before he audibly stated, "I'll be back."

"Did you say something?" Charlie asked me.

"I didn't," I said standing up to close the door behind Marlo since he nosily left it open. "That was a colleague that I just asked to leave my office."

"Ahh. Got it," he said without continuing.

"So, to what do I owe the pleasure of this phone call, Charlie?"

"I was waiting to get out of the earshot of Sabrina, sorry, Jax's mom. She asked a million questions in the elevator. All I could do was plead the fifth and tell her that I needed to talk to her husband first. Then she asked a question I didn't have the answer to."

"What question was that?" I inquired.

"She asked me why you called me Charlie." There was silence.

"Oh." *No. No. No. No. No* - my internal thoughts hounded me. "I slipped."

"It's not a big deal. It hadn't even crossed my mind until she asked." He was calm.

I chuckled at the thought of the 3rd degree he must have received in the elevator, "Oh gosh. I'm so sorry."

"Hey," another pregnant pause filled the air. It was almost like he was trying to decide what to say next. "I'm really glad you answered the phone. I was expecting to leave a voicemail for you."

"You were?"

"Yeah, I had my whole spiel planned out and everything."

"Well, run it by me!"

"Right now?"

"Sure, why not?" Marlo peeped his head into

the window of my office door and made faces mocking the fact that I was still on the phone with Charlie, the Mystery Man.

Charlie hesitated. "Okay. You're going to have to pretend like you're the voicemail message though, but I'll do it."

I jumped in without hesitation. "You've reached the voicemail of Dr. Chris. Unfortunately I'm away from my phone but if you'll leave your name, phone number, and a brief message, I'll get back to you at my earliest convenience. Happy Holidays! BEEP."

Have you ever heard someone smile through the phone? There's a shift in frequency. I've heard it before when I had my weekly phone calls with my parents, but my memory logged this as the first time I'd heard it from Charlie.

"Hi, Dr. Chris. It's Charlie Hughes. I was just in for a Check-up with my Godson, Jax. It was really good to bump into you again today, and I'm glad I can place a name to the face of the woman who's been running through my brain for the past week. I'd love to meet you for lunch or more cider someday soon. Feel free to give me a call at this phone number or on my landline. 816-555-1234. Yes, I have a landline, which pretty much makes me a dinosaur. Anyway, I look forward to speaking with you soon."

"Please push 7 to save this message or pound to re-record." He laughed. I inhaled, closed my eyes, and exhaled a smile. "So, what's your choice Charlie?" A beep echoed through the phone.

"I pushed 7."

"Good choice. My shift will be finished in about 30 minutes. Can I call you when I leave?"

"I'll be waiting for your call."

"Okay. I'll talk to you in a few."

"In a few."

We hung up the phone and I waved Marlo into my office, knowing full well that he had been watching from outside the entire time. Even further, knowing him, he was probably eavesdropping.

He walked in with an empty cup in hand, the eavesdroppers favorite tool.

"I knew it, Sneaky."

"So what'd he say?" Marlo was the nosiest

friend I had. But I knew his heart was in the right place. He was just watching out for me as he had since we were kids.

"I'm going to call him back when I'm out of earshot of my nosey friends," I told him with a sly smile.

"You had a lot more to say than that. I heard a voicemail greeting."

"I'll never tell," I said, my sly grin widening by the sentence.

"You will, after your phone call tonight."

"I will. After my phone call tonight." That was enough to appease Marlo.

"Okay, I'll leave you alone then. Talk to you later tater."

"Bye, Marlo. Can you close the door on the way out? I need to finish up these entries for my patient so I can get out of here."

"You got it!"

As the door closed, my fingers typed at the speed of light, rushing to ensure that the work was accurate, but that I could get out of here before someone called in for their shift. I typed the last few words, saved the record, then double checked that it was saved in the appropriate location. I sprang from my desk, grabbed my bag and coat in my hands without placing them on, locked my office door, headed down the hallway, and said goodnight to the staff that was still present. It felt like it all happened in one swift movement. Fortunately for me, there was nobody present to stop me as I exited in haste. Before I knew it I was in my car, gathering my thoughts and was nearly home before I summoned the courage to make that phone call.

I dialed the phone number that Charlie had called from and it went straight to voicemail. I heard the beep and started to leave my message.

"Hi Charlie, this is..."

Charlie was chuckling on the other end. "I couldn't help myself."

"You need to stop," I said through laughter.

"I wanted to hear your best voicemail message but I couldn't keep a straight face."

"You're a mess."

"You think so?"

"Clearly," I said in jest while snickering at how quickly I fell for his prank.

"So are you free for the night?" he asked, still chuckling.

"I'm free for the weekend, which is completely rare for me." It was, especially during the holidays.

"That sounds major! What plans have you you made for yourself?" he was looking for an opening and I had two options. I could serve the opening on a silver platter or I could make him work for it. I'm ornery. You know what I did.

"Well, a little bit of this. A little bit of that," I told him, waiting to see if he'd ask anymore questions.

He did, "Is it a full plate?"

"No. I wasn't entirely sure that I wouldn't be picking up someone else's shift so I didn't plan anything." *What was I doing? Why did I tell him that?*

"Oh?" he asked with a slight inflection in his tone.

"I'll probably decorate around my condo

since I'll actually have the time to do so this weekend."

"Hmm," he scoffed, sounding disinterested.

"What's hmm?"

"Nothing. What day were you going to decorate your place?"

"Probably Saturday so I can rest and enjoy it on Sunday."

"Would you like to grab some lunch or cider tomorrow before you start decorating?"

"Yes," I blurted out before I could stop myself.

"Which one?" he asked, seeking clarification.

"Yes."

Another smile. I could hear it. I still don't know how that works, but I heard it. I asked him to hold for a moment while I entered my condo, to ensure I could do so safely.

"Thanks for waiting," I said.

"Sure thing. So how about we head back to the Fresh Corner; lunch at the Fresh Pantry followed by another hot cider at the Fresh Grind?"

"Sounds perfect," I replied.

"11:30? Beat the holiday crowds?"

"I'll meet you there, Charlie."

"Sounds good, Dr. Chris."

"You really don't have to call me doctor."

"I kind of like it though," he said, still smiling.

"Okay, Charlie. Whatever works for you."

"I'll see you tomorrow Dr. Chris."

"11:30, Charlie."

"Have a good night."

"You too."

We hung up the phone and I tossed myself backwards on the couch, kicking and wriggling. There was something about his voice that excited me. It was warm and genuine. Soft yet considerate. I felt comfortable being myself around him and I was so looking forward to tomorrow's lunch, and Christmas decorating. I would finally get to enjoy this time of year. As I was stretched out on the couch, hugging my phone and recounting Charlie's voice, my phone vibrated.

I was so startled that I tossed the phone in the air and shot upright. The phone was still ringing as I reached up to catch it. I assumed it was Marlo, calling me since I hadn't called him yet.

"Hello?" I said with a bit of snark in my tone.

"Dr. Chris?"

That gravelly voice did not belong to Marlo. Nope. It was Charlie.

"Hiiiii Charlie."

"Are you okay?" he laughed.

"Yes," I started. "I think I dozed and the phone startled me awake." Technically daydreaming counts as dozing, right? In my mind it does.

He responded with concern in his voice. "Oh, I'm so sorry. You've probably had a long day, huh?"

"I have, but it's quite alright. How can I help you?"

"I feel bad now that I know I woke you up."

"I'm awake now. What is it?"

"I-, I couldn't remember if I wished you a good night."

"So you wanted to hear my voice again?" I asked jokingly.

"Guilty," he replied sounding as if his shoulders were raised in shame.

"I'm looking forward to learning more about you tomorrow, Charlie."

"What would you like to know about me?"

"I'll ask tomorrow."

"What if I need to prepare in advance for my test?" he joked.

"You already have all the answers," I replied with confidence in his ability to tell me more about what drives him as a person.

"Are you sure you're not an educator?"

"I'm sure. That job is for people with nerves of steel."

"Says the good doctor," he said while laughing at his own joke.

"Touché."

"Okay, I need to get some beauty sleep," he joked again.

"Yes, you do. I need you fresh for our date tomorrow."

"Hmm. Our date? But we just officially met."

"We did. Let's count it for what it is."

"Our first date. Got it," he said more seriously than I had anticipated. "I hope you sleep well, Dr. Chris. I'll see you tomorrow. Wait."

"Hmm?"

"If this is a date, should I pick you up?"

"I don't know you like that, Charlie."

"Oh, I think you know me better than you think you do, Dr. Chris."

I suddenly had trepidations that I would mess this up. *Where did this man come from?*

"I will meet you at the Fresh Pantry at 11:30 tomorrow morning, Charlie. Wear something comfortable. I may need to walk off my lunch."

"Lunch and a stroll. As you wish madame."

I giggled. He genuinely made me giddy. *What was happening?* "Good night, Charlie."

"Goodnight, Dr. Chris."

"Sleep well, Charlie."

"You too, Dr. Chris."

"I will, Charlie."

"I will too, Dr. Chris."

"You're stalling mister."

"I just like hearing you say, Charlie. There's a little bit of twang in it when you say it."

"Did you just call me country?"

"No. It's cute," he tittered.

"We're still on the phone, sir."

"I'm waiting for you to say it again."

"Say what, Charlie?"

"There it is!" he muttered through a throaty chuckle that made me grin from ear to ear.

I felt like a teenager again. We couldn't get off of the phone.

"Charlie?"

"Yes, Dr. Chris?" I smiled every time he said my name.

"You have a good night, for real this time, okay?"

"I most definitely will," he replied.

"Okay."

"Okay," he stalled again.

"Hang up the phone, Charlie."

He offered a lifeline, "Count of three?"

"So silly! Count of three."

We counted. I didn't hang up. Neither did he. I had to explain myself.

"I can't hang up on you. It seems rude. You called me, you'll have to end the call."

"What if I'm not ready to yet?" he asked.

"Then you're about to listen to me brush my teeth and get ready for bed."

"Then we'll brush our teeth together."

"Suit yourself." I rose from the couch and shut off the lights in the living room before walking into the bathroom to brush my teeth. I could hear Charlie doing the same.

"I'm going to put you on mute while I brush my teeth," I told him.

"Same."

I brushed my teeth, smiling at the thought of the guy on the other end of the phone doing the same. I ran into the bedroom after rinsing, and changed into my sleep wear. Just as I was about to take the phone off of mute, I heard his voice again.

"I'm climbing into bed now."

I unmuted my phone, "Me too."

There's that smile again. I could hear it once more.

"What are you smiling about?"

"Who said I was smiling?" he said, sounding as though he were trying to stifle his smile.

"I can hear it, Charlie."

"Oh, okay."

"You're smiling again."

"So are you." He was right. I was, from ear to ear.

"I am," I said, affirming his thought before attempting to muffle a yawn.

"I better get off the phone so you can get some rest. I know you put in some long hours."

"As do you."

"Somehow I don't think the two compare. Seriously this time Dr. Chris. I'm going to hang up."

“Okay, Chaaaaaalie” I said in the midst of a yawn. “Oh, pardon me!” I said, embarrassed to be yawning during our call.

His voice softened, “Sweet dreams, good doctor.”

“Thank you, Charlie. I’ll see you tomorrow.”

“Roger that.”

I giggled again, “Good night.”

“Good night, beautiful.”

My eyes opened wide. *click* Did he realize that he said that? Maybe it came out because of a sleep induced stupor. Maybe it’s nothing.

Or maybe it was.

Chapter 6
Dr. Chris' Date

Yesterday was long, but the surprise that accompanied my last patient nearly erased all of the challenges. I had been day-dreaming about this man all week and had just about given up on seeing him again when suddenly there he was. There was something incredibly honest about this Charlie Hughes that rattled my nerves and intrigued my senses all at the same time. I could hardly contain my excitement about brunch or lunch today. I knew that I was going to enjoy his company today, but I needed to tell somebody about where I would be. Nobody better than Marlo, who was going to give me crap about not calling last night. Better late than never though, right? I picked up the phone and dialed his number, then waited for him to answer.

"So she's alive!" Marlo joked as he answered

the phone.

“Ha ha. I’m sorry Marlo.”

“So did you call him or did you chicken out?” Just as I was about to respond, he went ahead and answered for me. “You called him. That’s why you didn’t call me back isn’t it?”

“Well, yes and no.”

“How does that work?” he asked with sincerity in his voice.

“So I called him. We spoke. Then we got off the phone.”

“Where does the no come into play?”

“Well he called me back.”

“How quickly?”

“After a minute or so maybe?” I paused, listening to Marlo make inaudible comments on the other side of the line. “I actually thought it was you, so I answered the phone with a bit of sass.”

“I’m assuming you reeled it in though.”

"I did."

"So what was the verdict?"

"We're going to lunch today," I said with a hint of excitement in my voice.

"Oh you must have worked that phone call," he said, pride beaming through his words.

"The second one ended with me yawning goodnight."

"Hmmmm."

"Don't, Marlo."

"You've never told me that you've done that with anyone else before. Only me."

"I didn't plan for it," I said.

"Nobody ever does. So it's 10:30, are you getting ready for your date. Wait, is it a date or just a getting to know you thing?"

"I called it a date. He called it a date."

"So, it's a date. Are you getting ready for it?"

"I was trying to decide what to wear when

you called. We're supposed to be somewhat comfy. I told him that we might need to walk off lunch."

"You know it's cold outside today, right?"

"Oh shoot." I had forgotten.

"Yeah, so don't try to dress too cute now. You can't be making rounds and getting all of our patients sick because you wanted to ignore the fact that it's nearly winter."

"Okay, dad."

"You know what I'm saying, Chris. I know you."

"I know." And I truly did know what he was saying. That would be irresponsible of me to do, but you never get a second chance to make a first impression. Well, I suppose I had already made my first impression in scrubs and a coat. It just struck me that I looked a hot mess that night and he still didn't care.

"The Dr. Who, hoodie will be just fine ma'am."

"I gotta go, friend. We're meeting at 11:30 and I still need to hop in the shower."

"Code 10!" he shouted. "What were you doing answering the phone? Be careful. Have fun. Bye!"

"Bye!"

That was just the redirection I needed to get focused and think about the weather season that we're in. The high temperature was only supposed to reach 34 for the day and I had to plan accordingly. I laid out an outfit across my bed and threw down a couple of alternate choices because I never know what's going to fit from day to day. Then, off to a quick shower, pulled my hair back into a low afro bun, and bolted back into the bedroom to get dressed. It left me just enough time to take one look in the mirror, grab my keys and coat, and head down towards The Fresh Corner. I know we said 11:30, but it was a Saturday, during the holiday season, and there was no snow in the forecast today which meant traffic would probably be fairly high.

I was glad I left the house early as there were a couple of unexpected slow downs on the way. There's nothing worse than being late somewhere. As I was looking for a place to park I saw him heading into the cafe, all huddled up like it was cold outside. Good to see we're both on the same page when it comes to time.

I lucked up and found a spot just around the corner from where we were going to eat. It took me little to no time to walk back to the cafe. Butterflies fluttering on 10, I took a deep breath just before opening the door and exhaled slowly to steady my nerves as I stepped inside. As they normally did in the winter time, my glasses fogged up when the warm air of the restaurant hit my lenses. It took a split second before they cleared and I could see, but that gave my other senses a chance to shine. A fragrant aroma filled the air that I didn't remember smelling when I was in here last week.

When the fog faded, I looked around the waiting area. There were two couples with children, an older couple who appeared to be married, and a trio of teenage friends who were all waiting to be seated. They all smiled at me as I glanced in their direction in search of Charlie's familiar face, which appeared to be the only one that I could not see. Funny. I know I had seen him walking inside, but now he had disappeared into thin air. Before I could look away towards the faces in the restaurant, one of the couples nudged their child in my direction. She couldn't have been older than 5.

"Are you Dr. Chris?" she asked me.

I stooped down to her height to speak with

her after seeking visual permission from her parents, "I am."

She pulled a single winter honeysuckle stem from behind her back and giggled as she handed it to me. "This is for you."

"Oh, thank you. Where did you -" I noticed her pointing behind me so I turned around. Within each group of patrons waiting to be seated, there was a person who stood up to greet me with a single stem. If it were possible for me to blush, I would have been as red as a holly berry.

I thanked each of them for their stem of honeysuckle and looked to them for answers. I knew he was in there somewhere. By the time I made it around the waiting area, everyone was smiling from ear to ear, waiting for my next surprise - the host, who also had a stem of honeysuckle for me. I was having a hard time discerning real life from a possible dream but could feel my face getting warm. Maybe I was blushing after all. The host walked me back to the same booth in the corner where Marlo and I sat last Saturday for lunch. But this time was different. Each booth I passed, delivered yet another honeysuckle stem. At this point all I could do was laugh in embarrassment as I carried this bundle of deliciously scented honeysuckle back towards my fate.

"Here you are, Dr. Chris," the host said to me, abandoning me with this stranger who I assume everyone thought was about to propose to me. All eyes were on me as he grabbed me by the right hand and guided me into the booth seat, smiling an ornery smile the entire time.

"Well, hello, Dr. Chris!" he quipped.

"Charlie." My twang was thick when I was excited about something, which made him chuckle.

I imagined him laughing the same way since he was a child. So joyful and uninhibited. If I weren't already smiling, his laughter certainly would have pulled one out of me.

He was hiding something, I could tell. But I didn't know what it was until he maneuvered an object from behind his back before sitting down and asking me, "Would you like a place to put your flowers?"

I looked down to see a beautiful red glass vase, etched with Season's Greetings, and wrapped with a single white ribbon. I carefully placed each of the white blooming honeysuckle stems inside and before he took his seat, he placed a single light red carnation in the center. I shook my head, completely befuddled at what had just happened.

"I certainly wasn't expecting this. Thank you," I said, still grinning from ear to ear.

"You said this was a date. I bring flowers to a date."

"I did say it was a date, didn't I?"

He nodded.

"Is this a light red carnation?" I asked him.

"Admiration," he said plainly with a sincere look on his face.

"These smell amazing, Charlie. Where did you find them?"

"I have a bush of them growing in my backyard. I cut them this morning."

"Okay, I'll stop asking questions."

He shrugged.

"I know you're decorating for the holidays today. I wanted to add a bit of fresh festivity to the mix."

"So thoughtful." I was completely taken aback by the consideration that went into that.

He asked me about the rest of my night, and my morning and I asked about his. We ordered our food, both of us opting for French Toast and fruit. The conversation took some interesting twists and turns, winding from places he's lived to how he found his way to Kansas City.

"I took a leap of faith, moving for an opportunity to change my career and at the time, Oakley, the woman who paid for our cider last week, and I were dating. It was an easy decision really. I didn't have any roots in Chicago. At the very least, even if Oakley and I didn't work out, I still had Steve and Sabrina, and thank goodness. I needed to lean on their support when I saw Oakley with another man as I was going to pick up her engagement ring from the jeweler."

"I'm so sorry, Charlie. That had to be heart-wrenching."

"It was. I was really salty for a while. Mad at the world and then after consulting with a few wise souls, I let it go. I realized that I was continuing to allow it to happen to me again and again, the longer I held onto it. Then when I released it-" he paused and smiled at me, "there you were."

I could feel half of a wall going up. Was I going to be a rebound? It's impossible to guard your heart and be open to something powerful simultaneously. But it's so hard not to guard your heart when your mind goes into self-defense mode. My facial expression must have told the tale of my internal turmoil.

"I'm sorry. I don't know why I told you all of that on a first date. I'm not even sure why I felt that comfortable doing so. That was actually pretty selfish of me. I'm sorry."

"It was honest. I appreciate that."

He nodded in thanks, as though he needed to hear that it was okay for him to share such personal information with me.

"Enough about me, Dr. Chris. Talk to me about you. How did you get into pediatrics?"

I shared my backstory with him and we spoke for a while about that, between shared bites of french toast. It felt like my soul had known his forever. There was an ease about the way in which we connected that I was having trouble explaining. But the longer we talked, the more that pony wall fell down until it was no longer existent again. We had just finished thanking the waiter for clearing our plates when I gazed over at my flowers and how they were catching the afternoon sun. I smiled, knowing that every time I looked upon them my heart would remember this day. I leaned over, eyes closed, and inhaled their essence which reminded me of Christmas time at my grandmother's house. I could see her playing carols at the piano and singing again, and me sitting right beside her singing in harmony. I could feel my emotions stirring within. This man had just given me a gift much deeper than even he was aware.

"Hey, are you okay?" Unbeknownst to me, he had been watching me the entire time, and saw my face morph from a smile to longing for a time long past.

A partial smile slid up on the right side of my face and I nodded. He could see I was not yet ready to speak, but didn't know it was for fear of shedding a tear or two. He reached across the table and opened his hands up to welcome mine. I studied his palms before giving in to complete vulnerability and placing my hands inside his. He squeezed them and looked me in my eyes. Not at them, into them, in search of the answer to his next question.

"What is it, Dr. Chris?"

"The flowers," I said, struggling to get any

additional words out.

"Was it too much?" A look of concern was strewn across his face.

"They," I swallowed down the lump in my throat. "They reminded me of Christmases with my grandmother."

He didn't know how to respond. His eyebrows raised in the center. His bottom lip tucked into his mouth. His thumbs traced over the trail of my knuckles in an attempt to comfort me.

"You want to tell me about her on our walk?"

"I would love to."

We sat fixed like that in silence while we waited for the waiter to bring the check. Charlie paid for our meal and helped me with my coat, then carried the vase of flowers out of the restaurant for me. His family had raised a gentleman and everyone in the restaurant knew it.

"We probably should've figured out where we were walking before we stepped out into the cold."

I nodded, then shivered, and offered an

option.

"I just parked around the corner. We can sit in my car to figure out the game plan if you'd like."

"Mmm hmm," he mumbled, afraid to bare his teeth to the nip of the air.

We walked expeditiously down the sidewalk and hung a right as he tried to guess which car was mine.

"The beamer?"

"Nope."

"Silver luxury vehicle?"

"Try again."

"That big truck with the reindeer nose on it?"

"No, Charlie." I walked up to the door of my car and pulled on the handle twice, which unlocked all of the remaining doors. We quickly hopped inside, out of the bite of the late fall air.

"I would not have guessed this vehicle at all," he said, looking around at the interior. "I see you Dr. Chris."

Ignoring his shenanigans, I asked him if he would strap the vase into the back seat.

"Strap it in?"

"Yes, buckle it with the seat belt and adjust the child safety strap if you can reach it."

"But if I do that from here then you'll see - "

"I've already seen it."

"I knew you were watching me walk away," he joked. "I could feel it!"

I smiled sheepishly.

He hopped out of the car and ran to the back door to secure the flowers in place before returning to the front passenger seat. I thanked him. He nodded through another shiver.

"So where are we walking?" he asked with a crooked smile.

"Umm. Is there a place indoors that will work?" We laughed in unison, then laughed at our laughter.

"I know a place that's not entirely indoors, but it has a bit more protection from the wind."

"That sounds good to me," I said. "Are we driving to it or walking to it?"

"We can either drive to it or take the streetcar there."

I looked at him as we noticed the streetcar making its exit just a block away from my car. "The next one will be here in ten minutes."

"Hey Iris," he started directing his words to his phone, "set a five minute timer." Iris affirmed that the timer was set.

So we sat, for four minutes, in the warm vehicle, watching people scurry by with holiday cheer. They carried bags, held hands, carted children, and genuinely seemed to be merry as they went about with their lives.

He looked at his phone to check the timer and noticed that we only had a minute left of warmth and comfort before we needed to make a dash to meet the next streetcar. Then panic appeared to set in.

"You wouldn't happen to have a blanket in the car with you, would you?" he looked serious, so I replied accordingly.

"Every good midwesterner keeps a bag of

warm, weather gear in their vehicle during the cold months."

"So every month except for July, and August then?" he asked.

I pointed back towards the trunk with my thumb just as Iris sounded an alarm for us to make the trek to the streetcar.

On the count of three we hopped out of the warmth and met at the back of the vehicle. I ducked into the trunk, pulling out and handing him the wool blanket that I kept in case of an emergency. He laughed at the size of it.

"This thing could fit a twin size bed!"

"Full size bed," I said with a smile while watching him duck his head in towards his shoulders as the wind whipped by us again. That's when I noticed that he didn't have a scarf on. Hat, gloves, coat - yes. It was 30 degrees outside. I dipped back into my bag in the trunk.

"What are you doing?" he asked. "We need to head towards..."

I leaned back out, closed the trunk, then wrapped a scarf around his neck to keep him warm. With his hands still holding the blanket, there was nothing he could do to stop me. So instead he smiled, looked at me as if to ask where I had come from, then said, “thank you.”

I locked the car doors and we hustled towards the street car stop. When we reached the intersection, he instinctively grasped for my hand which I took hold of - for safety purposes, right? That’s what I told myself anyway as we crossed the street hand in hand, off to our next adventure.

I wasn’t even sure where we were going. He hadn’t told me and I, oddly enough, did not ask. The street car wasn’t in sight when we got to the stop, but there were loads of people waiting behind the weather shield which had been festively adorned with green wreaths filled with red ribbons and ornaments for the holidays. There was just enough room behind the shield for one more person, so he guided me into safety from the wind’s wrath. But before he could let go, I tugged on his hand, bringing him in with me. There wasn’t room for us to stand side by side, but we could both fit if we stood one in front of the other. So there we were, him in front of me facing the street, holding the blanket with his left arm and lacing his gloved fingers in between those on my right hand. I stepped closer to him, closing the gap between us and resting my forehead on his back to block more of the wind.

He leaned his head over his right shoulder, "Are you cold?"

My stomach clenched repeatedly from the frigid temperatures, causing me to begin bouncing up and down like everyone else who was waiting for the streetcar. "I am."

He wrapped my right arm around his midsection and tucked it under the blanket to warm me up. I know we had just met, but I didn't hesitate for even half of a moment as he pulled me closer. "Where's your other hand, Dr. Chris?" he asked while reaching back for me. I felt well attended to and cared for. Shoot, I felt downright adored. I offered him my left hand, and without realizing it, a small piece of my heart too.

Part of me was sad to see the arrival of the streetcar as I knew it meant that this temporary embrace of necessity was coming to an end. Just as the car pulled to a stop, I squeezed him closer and glanced up at him, chin on his back. He looked back at me with a smile that spoke a million words, patted the top of my hands, swayed slightly from side to side, then guided me safely onto the streetcar.

Chapter 7
Charlie's Date

She squeezed me like she didn't want to let go, and I looked down and caught a peek of her striking brown eyes. So much life in there. I hadn't expected it, but the cold weather had added a layer of complexity to this date that I greatly appreciated. It brought us closer, literally and emotionally. I discovered something I didn't know was missing until it was suddenly available to me. I helped her onto the streetcar before joining her.

There weren't any seats available on our car, so we were forced to stand. Part of me preferred it that way because I got to watch her study and admire the decorations that lined Main Street. Each store front window was decorated with red and tinsel, or green and gold. I could tell that she loved this time of year by the way her face lit up. It was like she was absorbing as much of this moment as her memory would allow her to hold. She couldn't see it, but I spent more time watching her than looking at all of the sights of the city. I was trying hard to stay present, but my mind was starting to wander off into the future.

Suddenly she turned to face me, "So what's our stop, Charlie?"

I tried to be cool about it. "We're riding to the City Market. Just a few more stops now."

"Got it."

At the next stop more people boarded our section of the streetcar. It was starting to get over crowded. So I asked if she wanted to get off sooner or if she wanted to ride all the way to our stop. She opted for the crowded warmth.

Once our stop arrived, I hopped off in front of her to give her my hand as she stepped off the car. We walked around and took in all the scents of the market; spices from around the world, different roasts of coffee, sweet treats, and food of all types. There were craft vendors selling their handmade goods and we roamed from section to section browsing their wares. We found farm sourced honey and shared an inside joke when we saw someone selling winter honeysuckle.

Moving from aisle to aisle took a little over an hour with us stopping to chat with the vendors and in between those conversations, chatting about her grandmother, until it was almost too cold to do so.

"Are you ready to hop back on the streetcar?" I asked her.

"Sure." We walked towards the stop, chatting along the way.

"Have you sufficiently burned off your lunch?"

She hesitated before asking, "Could we hop off at Union Station?" There was excitement in her voice and a twinkle in her eyes. I could tell she really wanted to stop there and I had no plans of stopping her.

"As long as you're good on time. We're coming up on 3 o'clock."

"I have all weekend," she replied, looking me dead in my eyes.

"Do I get all weekend?" I asked her, slowing my stride down so as to not out pace her.

"I mean, you're on winter break aren't you? You have what, two weeks? Three weeks?"

"I meant with you." It had come out of my mouth before I could stop it and now I was afraid of her reply.

"You want all weekend?" She asked, eyes still fixed on my gaze.

I rolled my shoulders back and tried to stifle a smile. "Don't ask me that." She laughed at my anguish. I don't think she truly understood the struggle. It was different hearing that question come out of her mouth than it would have been had she just answered my question when I asked it initially.

"You asked me. I was just seeking clarification." She was right. I started that. I only had myself to blame for that one.

Sabrina Effect.

Steve would be so excited that the good doctor and I were getting along so well. He knew I was ready before I did.

"You're right," I said. "Also, you don't have to answer that question."

"Let's see where the day leads us," she replied with a reassuring smile before turning her attention back to the walk towards the street car stop. Again, there was barely room for us to squeeze out of the path of the wind, but people kindly made room for her. I wanted to give her some space so I stood directly on the other side of the plexiglass. She only had to shiver once for me to realize that my plan was not going to work out as I had hoped. I stepped back in front of her and apologized for leaving her to fend for herself. I handed her the blanket and slid behind her, wrapping my arms through the fold of the blanket and around her waist to keep her warm.

"Is this okay?" I asked her. No words were spoken. I thought maybe she hadn't heard me so I leaned in and asked it again, closer to her ear.

"Is this okay?" Still no words from Dr. Chris.

She replied by resting her head against my left shoulder. I was hoping that I had on enough layers of clothing to mask the sound of my heartbeat because it was working overtime at that moment.

This woman.

The streetcar rounded the corner and made its presence known, so I squeezed her the same way she had squeezed me, and mockingly placed my chin upon the top of her head which got the reaction I was looking for - a ginger chuckle.

The two of us boarded the street car, which had ample room for us to sit down this time around. So we sat, her beside the window and me on the aisle. I draped the blanket across our legs and stretched my right arm across the back of the seats in which we sat.

As the streetcar rumbled its way through downtown and headed towards Union Station, I started daydreaming, thinking back to this morning as I had rushed around to prepare for our date.

I woke up excited about the possibility of what could be as a result of this day. She asked for it to be a date and I wanted to make sure it was one worth remembering. Knowing she was about to decorate her place for Christmas, I had a flowering bush in my backyard that was in bloom with winter honeysuckle. I thought they could add a festive element to her place, and it was like giving her a part of me to remember. I ran outside and snipped a few stems, then trimmed them down to a height that wouldn't tower over her head. I had a friend who told me about a florist that was willing to sell just a vase without flowers. I swung by there on my way to the Fresh Corner and picked one up, along with a single light red carnation to symbolize how much I admired her. Then the plan was on.

Because I stopped at the florist, I was a bit behind schedule so I hoped that she wouldn't be waiting for me at the cafe when I arrived. Luckily she wasn't. So I explained my plan to the wait staff, and they helped me ask customers if they would be willing to make this a special date for Dr. Chris. I didn't have a single person turn down my request.

Her face as she arrived was priceless. She looked both stunned as well as a bit confused. She had to know I was behind it, but she couldn't see me yet. I don't know if the best part was watching her search for me or getting to see the look of joy (and slight embarrassment) on her face with the delivery of each honeysuckle branch. I watched her face turn red, which was hard for us to do. Her joy brought me joy and her excitement would be seared on my mind for a long time to come. I guess that was probably the best part. I see now why Steve has voluntarily flipped for Sabrina over and over and over again.

This woman.

She had noticed that I was shivering at the car and made it a point to take care of me, wrapping a scarf around my neck without even so much as asking me if I needed it. She probably knew I would refuse. Machismo was a strange thing. We'll freeze before we let someone know that we're cold. But Dr. Chris, she knew what I needed, and how to make sure that I was taken care of before even I knew what I needed.

I was in trouble and I smiled at the thought of it.

"What are you thinking about over there mister?" She asked, catching me in my reverie.

"Today." *Why was I so honest with her about everything?*

She smiled in return, and turned her attention back out the window, placing her hands on top of her lap, and the blanket. I dropped my left hand on top of the blanket between us and opened it, palm up. She dropped her left hand on top of mine and we rode the rest of the way in silence, my heart growing larger with each passing block.

There were a total of 8 stops before we hit Union Station and I knew that she and I would have to get up eventually. So I looked towards the world outside our streetcar window and took it all in; the people, the stores, the atmosphere, Dr. Chris, everything. If this was what the holidays could be like, I wanted to take part in them.

We de-boarded at Union Station and I

asked her where we were headed. She pointed to a poster of the grand hall, which was just beyond the humongous Christmas Tree. While I marveled at its height, she asked a stranger if they could take a photo of the two of us in front of the tree, then handed them her phone when they gladly obliged. All of the sudden I panicked. *How do we stand?*

"Dr. Chris, are you posing us?"

"One silly and one regular?"

"Silly first then."

The kind stranger was snapping away unbeknownst to us. We posed for two, then thanked her before looking at the pictures. She captured some great candid photos of the two of us chatting with each other before striking our best silly pose - a b-boy stance, of course, and then standing side by side, with one arm around each other. But my favorite was the one just before that. We were gazing into each others eyes, communicating how we should stand for the last posed picture and it's one of the most natural looking photos I've ever seen. It looked almost exactly like a photo I had taken of Steve and Sabrina before their first date was over. She paused on that photo for half a minute and added it to her favorites folder.

We hot footed it to the Grand Hall in search of what we had seen on the poster. Dr. Chris just stood and admired the beauty of it all. Children posing in the giant sleigh with their siblings and cousins, some running around and listening to the echo of their voices in the towering ceilings. Snowflakes of varying sizes hung from the ceiling at different heights. There was a child-sized Christmas themed train ride that kids waited to ride, and model train sets near the back of the Grand Hall that had been decorated for the holidays as well. Even I felt the Christmas spirit being in there.

Dr. Chris and I pointed out all the tiny details that people had included within the different train sets whose tracks were woven together. It was a mini winter wonderland and I felt like a child again. We walked through the entire train town which was packed with children darting in and out of the tiniest spaces, and people generally not watching where they were walking because they were so mesmerized. I extended a hand for Dr. Chris while we were in there and we guided each other through the rest of the space together. One pair of siblings even used us as a drawbridge, running between us and underneath our arms. I hadn't enjoyed myself like this in a while.

"Are you hungry at all?" Dr. Chris asked with

a facial expression that looked like she was secretly hoping the answer was yes.

"Yes."

"Let's take the skywalk to Monarch Square. There are quite a few options over there."

"I'm game."

I was expecting her to let go of my hand once we left the train exhibit but she didn't. Instead, we walked back through the Grand Hall, up the stairs and over to the skywalk which vaulted us above the city streets in a warm glass cocoon pathway that protected us from the weather.

We stopped to share an order of truffle fries at a cafe just inside the shopping center. Neither of us wanted much to eat. Only enough for us to have the stamina to keep going. So we snacked on the fries and did some more people watching between conversation about her favorite part about Christmas in Kansas City.

"The people. I always love watching how much hope there is in people's eyes during this time of year." She nodded in my direction, "Yours are no exception." I looked away in protest.

This woman.

We took the elevators up to the second floor and listened to a children's choir sing Christmas songs. I placed an arm around her as she was propped up on the hand rail, and leaned in to whisper, "The sun is about to set."

She turned to face me and we asked each other in unison, "Mayor's Christmas Tree?"

It was just across the street from Monarch Square and immediately beside the Ice Rink.

We hustled down the escalator and out the front doors of the center, stepping outside just in time to see the lights of the Christmas Tree and surrounding area turn on.

"Perfect," she said, glancing around and taking it all in.

That word hung out in my ear as the sun continued its descent in the night sky. As much as I didn't want it to end, I knew that Dr. Chris had plans for today and I felt like our extended date had encroached on that.

"It's getting late, Dr. Chris. I owe you a hot cider."

Her head dipped as she nodded and bit her lower lip.

"You're right."

"You're supposed to be decorating your place for the holidays."

"I did say that didn't I?"

"You did."

"But you do owe me some cider. Actually, I owe you some cider for last week."

"You don't owe me a thing. Let's head back to the skywalk so we can catch the streetcar."

We made the trek back through the shopping center, over the skywalk cocoon and back to Union Station just in time to catch a waiting streetcar. The families who had filled the street car before were all headed in other directions for the day, which left the two of us on a car together with the operator and a jazz band playing holiday music.

"I'll be right back," I told Chris, heading in the direction of the band as the streetcar exited Union Station.

She watched with suspicion as I whispered to the jazz band members and pointed in her direction, them nodding and smiling in response to our conversation.

The drummer gave us a high hat roll and the keyboardist gave us a soft intro that sounded familiar to Dr. Chris. I walked back towards the location where she chose a seat and caught the eye of the streetcar operator who started humming just as I invited Dr. Chris to leave the blanket in the seat and stand up and dance with me. The operator began singing, as I helped her up to slow dance.

"Maybe I'm crazy to suppose
I'd ever be the one you chose,
out of a thousand, invitations, you'd receive.
oh but in case I stand one little chance
here comes the jackpot question in advance
What are you doing New Year's, New Year's Eve?"

She looked up at me as we danced and I raised an eyebrow to seek her answer.

"Let me check my calendar." We laughed together and danced as the streetcar carved its way back to our stop. The band finished, just as we arrived and instead of us cheering them, we were the ones receiving the applause. The band knew this was our first date. I'd told them as much. The streetcar operator did not. After we had retrieved the blanket and were about to exit,

Dr. Chris and I thanked her for the serenade.

"Don't ever stop loving each other," she said in reply.

We exited the streetcar hand in hand, in silence. We walked to the Fresh Grind, in silence. We stood in line, in silence until it was time to order.

"Two hot ciders, each with a spoonful of sugarplums, and one with a," she tapped me on the arm, "both with a dash of cinnamon extract."

"Is that for here or to go?" we were asked.

I looked in her eyes in search of an answer and instead found it in the corners of her mouth.

"To go," I said, looking at her for confirmation. She nodded.

Oakley greeted both of us and this time accepted my payment.

We grabbed some extra napkins and left the Fresh Grind, opting instead to stand in the cold night air with our warm ciders. The words of the street car operator stuck with me and I could tell that Dr. Chris was having a hard time with it as well.

"So that was great until it got kind of awkward," I said breaking the tension. She laughed.

"I still don't know what to say about it," she replied.

"Don't say anything about it," I told her.

She couldn't. "I've never had anyone say that to me. Have you ever had someone say that to you?"

I paused, only for a breath, "No."

Silence filled the air again so I cut it with another poignant stab at a joke. "But she had a beautiful voice though."

"She did indeed," another pregnant pause filled the air. "It was all so unexpected."

"What part?" I asked.

"The entire day, Charlie." Her tone was serious. "This. Whatever this is, I wasn't prepared for you." There it was again. Silence. I didn't know what she meant by that and I was afraid to ask. So I said the only thing that came to mind.

"Let me walk you to - "

She continued before I could finish my statement. "I wasn't prepared for you, but here we are, on our first date, and I have to be honest." *Oh no, honesty was a scary thing coming from women*. "I don't want to go decorate my place just yet."

Oh, well that wasn't so bad.

"What would you like to do?" I asked.

"I just want to spend some more time with you, if that's okay."

"I have an idea," I told her. "Do you trust me?"

She wrapped her arm around mine, looked me square in my eyes and took a deep breath, "Let's go."

This woman.

Chapter 8
Kansas City Christmas Challenge

As the two of us walked, he asked if I would be more comfortable driving or if I would be okay with him at the wheel. Not knowing where we were going, I decided that it would be much better for me to at least have a little bit of control over something.

"I'll drive if you're willing to give me directions," I said.

We did an about face and instead walked in the direction of my car. I popped the trunk so he could place the blanket in the back on the way to the passenger's side. He closed the trunk and smiled at me, carrying it into the car with him and buckling his seatbelt.

"So here's the plan," he started. "A Kansas City Christmas Challenge."

My body shifted positions, shoulders facing his direction and left hand draped across the steering wheel. "I'm intrigued."

A smirk graced Charlie's face, "We've already started it. But I'm going to share a list of Kansas City Christmas Traditions with you via phone."

"Okay."

He created a note and added my phone number to the list of who can see and edit it. My phone alerted me to a new message which prompted me to glance down at the screen and read the name of the list. It brought an immediate smile to my face, "Dr. Chris and Charlie's Spoonful of Sugarplums."

"I got it, but it's empty."

"I want us to create the list together before we take off to the next place."

"I like it."

"We don't have to get to all of them tonight, or even period if the list is really long."

"Save some for next Christmas, got it," I said nodding and typing an activity into the list before realizing what I had said. *Why did I say that?* Maybe he hadn't heard me.

Without missing a beat he finished, "But let's see if we can get as many as possible before Christmas."

"That's 4 days from now, and we have all day tomorrow too. Let's do it!" I had butterflies in my stomach from the excitement of this challenge. Our challenge.

Charlie's face was dancing the tango. I don't even know if he was aware of the face he was making, so I asked him what was going on.

"I didn't know I was making a face."

I swirled my pointer finger encircling the outline of his head, "You're still making the face."

"You said we have all of tomorrow."

"I did. Asked and answered."

He shook his head at me again, as if he were wondering where I came from. What he didn't know is that I was wondering the exact same thing about him.

"So about this list," I asked him. "What are some of the general Christmas traditions that you'd like to keep?"

We traded a list of things to do including:

- decorating the house
- baking and gifting cookies
- spending time with framily
- picking out a Christmas tree
- visiting Union Station
- visiting Monarch Square
- getting hot cider
- ice skating
- a carriage ride on the Plaza
- Mayor's Christmas Tree visit

We started there, but because of how he set up the shared checklist, the two of us could cross off items as we did them and add more if there was something we thought of at the time.

I crossed off the Mayor's Christmas Tree visit, visiting Union Station, and visiting Monarch Square.

"The way I see it," Charlie said, "we can ice skate on a day when it's warmer. But we have this perfectly good blanket and we can head to the plaza for a carriage ride now if you'd like. That would be a great way to end this date and it leaves us something to do tomorrow."

I buckled my seat belt and put the car in drive then we headed for the Plaza. The multicolored holiday lights that were strung along the tops and corners of each and every one of their 18 buildings lit up the cold night sky. We lucked up and found a parking spot on the street, then made it to the carriage ride kiosk in time for us to catch a ride in the carriage that was shaped like Cinderella's.

Charlie helped me into the tall-rise step, and handed me the blanket. When he hopped up inside with me, the carriage driver introduced himself to us and asked if we were on a date night.

"Our first date night," Charlie replied quickly, hoping to thwart off any potentially awkward comments like we had received earlier today.

The driver turned back around and looked at the two of us, bouncing his head back and forth between Charlie and I. "Really?" he asked with astonishment in his voice.

"Really, really," Charlie and I said in unison.

The driver chuckled. "Are you sure about that?" he asked, turning back around with a knowing smile before signaling the horses to giddy-up.

I draped half of the blanket over Charlie's legs, keeping the other half on my own. The driver offered to play us some Christmas tunes and we accepted. When he turned on his radio, a familiar song began to fill the crisp night air.

A soft soulful crooner piped out the lyrics, "What are you doing New Year's, New Year's Eve?"

I scooted closer to Charlie and snuggled up beside him. He wrapped his arm around me and tucked the blanket behind me to block the wind and keep me warm. I rested my head on his shoulder, and in doing so let my fears float away. He rested his cheek on the top of my stocking cap covered head, relaxing into the seat. I didn't know where we were about to go, but I knew in my gut that we would be going together. The challenge wasn't in trusting him, it was in trusting my own discernment. I had a stellar track record when it came to applying discernment on the job, but within relationships, I shortchanged myself consistently. I knew there was a tall hill to climb in terms of personal growth, but I was confident that it was a hill that was worth putting in the work to achieve.

The lights were beautiful. I was snuggled up beside a man who was caring and considerate. Then before I forgot to do so, I pulled out my phone and took a picture of the carriage driver and horse, the all white twinkle lights surrounding structure of our cinderella carriage, and eventually a couple of selfies of Charlie and I - one silly, one regular. In terms of first dates, I don't think it would be possible to top this. But from what I know of this mystery man, whose presence has become even more mysterious to me, he would absolutely try to top it. Our horse drawn tour took 30 minutes. People in cars took pictures of us, as their children, whose eyes grew wide in awe, waved at us like we were royalty. We smiled at them and waved back.

"I think we just became a Christmas memory for that child," he said. The thought of that reminded me of the first time I saw a family riding in these as a child. I had vowed to my 5 year-old self that one day I would take my own family on a carriage ride like this.

One car pulled up beside us and seemed to be pacing the speed of the carriage, which was being pulled by two trotting horses, so you can imagine how slow we were going. I finally looked over when I heard a knocking sound on one of the car windows. And there was a child, elementary school aged, waving and pointing at Charlie.

"I think this child wants to get your attention."

He turned his face in the direction of the car and laughed as the passenger window rolled down and a woman spoke up, "So sorry, he wouldn't let us go home without saying hi!"

She rolled down the back window for him and the child stuck his arm out of the car to wave, shouting, "Mr. Hughes! Mr. Hughes! Merry Christmas!!"

Waving and chuckling, Charlie joyfully shouted back, "Merry Christmas, Joel!"

Just before the car pulled off, Joel, waved at me, and nodded back at Charlie, giving him the thumbs up. Even the carriage driver had a good laugh about that one.

Charlie explained to me that Joel was one of his current students and I watched his whole demeanor light up as he spoke about his talents in writing. In one of our conversations from earlier in the day he mentioned that he wasn't sure if his decision to switch to education was the right one, but I knew by the way in which he spoke about Joel that he was right where he belonged.

The conversation shifted as the carriage ride was coming to an end, and we talked about which items we'd tackle tomorrow, and a good time to meet again to finish up the list before Christmas. The carriage driver helped us both out of the cinderella cage and I saw Charlie tip him on his way out. We thanked him for the great experience and he piped up, "We'll see you two next year."

These people didn't understand how much pressure they were laying on us, with the predictions and prophecies they were giving.

Nervously laughing it off, Charlie offered to take a ride share service back to his car, but I insisted on driving him. So with our ride complete, and another Christmas Challenge item complete, we took the scenic route back to the Fresh Corner area of the city, neither of us seeming to mind the extra time together. I relied on his guidance to get me back to his car, which turned out to be a blue pickup truck that was parked directly in front of the Fresh Grind. I lucked up on a spot immediately beside his vehicle and placed the gear in park.

"I can put this in the back for you if you'd like," he said, holding up the blanket that now held a memory all its own.

"Thank you." I nodded, watching him exit my car and slowly walk to the rear of my vehicle, knowing with certainty that I would see him again tomorrow, which eased the ache in my soul of parting ways for the day.

I popped the trunk for him and his feet seemed to drag, which he hadn't done all day. I saw him place the blanket back in the car, and return to the driver's side window with my old stethoscope.

"I think you need to use this, Dr. Chris," he said while looking at me intently.

"Why is that, Charlie?" I asked with urgency, wondering if he was suffering a medical emergency.

He handed me the stethoscope and I put it on, placing the earpieces in my ear canals and holding the chest piece in my hand. He unzipped his coat, then guided my hand and the chest piece to his heart and held them both there. "Just listen."

I could hear the whooshing sound of his heartbeat rising and falling, faster and faster. I looked up into his eyes and listened as his heart rate continued to increase. I removed the chest piece from his chest, and took the earpieces out of my ear. I rolled up the window and left the stethoscope inside the car before stepping out and into both the cold and his warm embrace.

We held onto each other in the cold, neither of us wanting to let go but both of us aware that at some point we'd have to. I closed my eyes to paint a picture of this day for my memory banks and listened as he hummed the tune that had followed us around. We held our embrace and swayed in the wind for what felt like an hour, though in reality it was only just a few minutes, breaking it only when his cell phone buzzed in his pocket.

"I need to check this in case it's my parents," he spoke softly.

He looked at the phone, saw the number and turned his head in the direction of the Fresh Grind. Oakley. He held the phone up for her to see that he was ignoring the call and placed it back in his pocket before turning his attention back to me.

"I need to go before I'm too sleepy to drive, Charlie," I told him.

He asked if he could call me when he got home. I agreed to it and we hugged once more, just long enough to get in one squeeze before parting ways. What a first date. I could hardly believe what I had just experienced, but I knew that I needed to journal about it before I forgot or before the events of the day became distorted with time. We returned to our respective cars and got buckled in. He waited until I had backed out of the parking spot before backing out of his. He had delivered on his promise of a date for sure, but the call at the end of the night raised a bit of a flag with me. I hoped that it was nothing, but I wasn't sure what to trust. I know I said I was working on my discernment, but that takes work and time, time and work. With both, I would be able to trust my gut and ensure that I wasn't making impulse decisions and disguising them in the name of discernment. That never works.

I drove to my condo and rushed inside. The doorman greeted me with questions, "Dr. Chris! Late shift at the hospital tonight?"

"I'm off this weekend, Ralph!"

"Oh! Well I hope you enjoy your time away."

"So far so good!" I said, a smile beaming across my face.

I called Marlo on my way home, but the call went to voicemail. I left a message providing scant details of the date and giving him an out not to call me tonight. As soon as I stepped off the elevator my phone rang. I knew it was Marlo, ignoring my message and calling me back.

"What man?" I answered, walking down the hallway to my door.

Charlie laughed on the other end of the phone. "So that's what we're doing?"

I really did need to start checking the callerID before answering the phone. This was getting dangerous.

"Sorry, Charlie. I thought it was someone else calling me."

There was silence on the other end of the phone. I hoped my comment hadn't left him with any doubt about how much I enjoyed the day so I started to speak, at the same time as Charlie.

Both of us starting with the same word, "I -"

"Go ahead," I told him, unlocking the door to my place and stepping inside. I placed my keys and the flowers on the table in my entryway.

"No, you go ahead. Ladies first," he said.

"Okay. I'll just be over here waiting in silence while you say what you were going to say," I told him.

Silence filled the air of my condo. No lights

on, no television, no radio, just open blinds with a view of the lights of Kansas City that drowned out the stars. I waited, just as I said I would.

Finally, he spoke. "So Chris, I'm sorry about the way the night ended."

"What do you mean?" I asked, seeking clarification on what he meant versus what I heard him say.

"The phone call from Oakley. The two of us embracing outside of her coffeehouse. It hadn't crossed my mind where we were at the time. I was so focused on how I was feeling that I didn't consider how you might feel about that."

"Oh. It didn't cross my mind until she called. Then it wandered all over the place. In fact, most of the ride home was spent thinking about all of the questions I had and where they were coming from. Then I realized, we've only had one date and I was questioning things that someone in a relationship would question. I told myself, if it were something that needed explaining, you would explain it, and all of my worries danced away."

"So what types of questions did you have?"

"Don't worry about them Charlie."

"I'm not worried about them, but I don't want to leave them unanswered. You and all of your compassion, joy, strength, and intelligence deserve that."

I was stuck on stupid for a moment, not knowing what to say. It was my heart that needed the stethoscope this time.

"Charlie," I began softly, "you don't owe me any answers to any questions."

"She left me a message, Chris."

"Who did?" I knew who he was talking about. Again - clarification.

"Oakley did. I listened to it as we drove away from our date. She was heated, then it struck me that it might have looked like I was parading you around to shove it in her face. But I need you to know that today didn't have anything to do with her."

I didn't have anything to say.

"Today was the first day I ever fully opened myself up for what could be. I mean ever. I've always held back a small part of me in case there was a chance that the other person would leave, I guess so it wouldn't hurt as bad. But I asked myself this morning when I woke up, what I might receive if I instead poured my entire heart into something, if I was truly open. If I was willing to be honest and vulnerable. What would I lose in doing that? When I realized that I wouldn't lose anything, I went all in. And what I received in return from you was far greater than anything I could have imagined in my wildest dreams."

"Charlie," I attempted to speak, not realizing he wasn't yet finished.

"Thank you, Dr. Chris for affirming that for me." I paused, collecting my thoughts in a coherent bubble before sharing them with him.

"So when I bumped into you in the coffee shop, I couldn't figure out why I was so drawn to you, but it felt like you were the smooth talking type, so I bolted. I didn't trust myself with smooth talkers. I told my friend, Marlo, about you over lunch the next day and I saw you go into the coffee shop and sit down with Oakley. So the call, coupled with what I saw last Saturday, made me wonder if you were still together, or in the process of getting back together. Marlo tried to get me to go talk to you that day, and I thought I was content just letting it be what it was. But my heart wouldn't let it rest. I thought about you all week and I told myself, that the next time I saw you, I would at least introduce myself, unless of course you had a ring on your finger. Then there you were, yesterday, in the place I least expected you to be. So I introduced myself and left it at that."

"But I couldn't."

"You didn't let it."

He let out a sigh, seemingly in languish.

"I made a promise to myself to trust my gut instead of my head, and my gut was screaming that this would be okay. So I need you to understand that I'm working on that. I need you to understand that I wasn't looking for you. I need you to know that I'm glad you're here, and for what it's worth, I need you to understand that I'm going to trust myself first. So for however long this works, I'm open to growing to know more about you."

I heard that smile again.

"Okay smiley. Why so quiet?" I asked him.

He nearly whispered his words, "Just trying not to overthink this."

"Hey, I have something to send you. But I need to take a picture of it first to do that. Let me call you right back."

"You know you can just do that while -"

"Let me call you back, Charlie."

"Sure thing."

I took a picture of the table in my entryway, texted it to Charlie along with the words 'Thank You', then called him back on his landline.

"Dr. Chris?"

"Hello, Dino," I smirked. "So how often does this phone ring?"

"It's on the other end of the house, I had to run to the other room to answer it. The only other people that have this phone number are my parents."

"Oh. Sorry, I hope I didn't cause you to think it was an emergency."

"I wouldn't have given you this number if I didn't want you to use it. Wait, I didn't leave an actual voicemail with this number, did you write it down?"

"I have a mind like a steel trap, Charlie. Be

careful what you say around me," I teased.

"Duly Noted. So, the vase of flowers looks good on that table."

"That's in my entryway, so they'll put me in the holiday spirit whether I'm coming or going."

I could hear him tapping on the screen to make the photo larger, "Where's the carnation?" he audibly wondered.

"You'll have to see if you can find it when you help me decorate tomorrow."

"Oh. I thought we were going to meet for breakfast and plan the rest of the day from there."

"We can still do that, but decorating the house for Christmas was on the list wasn't it?"

"It was."

"And I believe it was you who said you should pick me up if it's a date, right?"

"You do have a solid memory. What time would you like to eat?"

I was so busy adding an item to the list that I

missed his question.

"Dr. Chris added an item to the list." He was reading a notification that had just come through. "Let's just see what she added." I snickered at his narration. "'Visit a Christmas Tree farm to get a tree.' Okay. I'll see your Christmas Tree Farm and raise you this."

I opened my tablet to review the notification from him. "Create two holiday wreaths from scratch."

"Do you know how to create a wreath from scratch?" I asked him, knowing full well that I had never attempted to create one myself.

"How hard can it be?" he asked.

"I'm sure there's a video we can watch online somewhere."

"Hey are you a football fan at all?"

"Oh shoot! I forgot that tomorrow is Sunday. We'd better go early so we can watch them play somewhere."

"How about this. Let's get up early and grab some breakfast. If you're open to it, I can pick you up around 7:30. It looks like there's a tree farm just across the state line in Kansas that opens at 9. We can take my pickup out there and find a tree, then take it back to your place to put it up and watch some football. Then play the rest by ear."

Charlie was just as much of a planner as I was. "That sounds good to me." I sent him the address to my condo via my tablet with some directions that said, "I live in a high rise building. The doorman's name is Ralph. I'm in unit 227. No, I'm not kidding."

I heard him chuckle after reading my message.

"I'll be at your door. Wait, will Ralph, let me do that?" he said somewhat jokingly.

"He will."

"Okay. I'll be at your door at 7:30, Dr. Chris."

"I'll see you in a few hours, Charlie."

"Sleep well, beautiful." I smiled, hearing him say it for the second night in a row.

"You too, Charlie. Good night."

"Good night."

I hung up the phone and surveyed my condo, ensuring that it was clean enough to invite company over and deciding it was. Then it struck me that we would probably be hungry when we got back from the tree farm, so I sent just one more quick message before getting ready for bed.

"Do you eat meat? If yes, would you like some homemade chili for lunch?"

His reply, "Yes, and only if it's good."

"If it's not good we can order a pizza."

I placed my phone on the table and proceeded to get ready for bed. After brushing my teeth and returning to close the blinds, I grabbed my phone and noticed I had a missed call from Marlo and a message from Charlie.

"Really looking forward to seeing you tomorrow."

I muted the screen, turned off the light in the bathroom and crawled into bed. Really looking forward to seeing him tomorrow too.

Chapter 9
Christmas Challenge Continued

I woke up late.

His words rolled around in the forefront of my mind. "I'll be at your door at 7:30."

It was 7:15. He was probably already on his way to get me. I sprang from my bed and bolted into the bathroom. I had just enough time to brush my teeth, hop in the shower and throw on some clothes before the intercom rang.

"Hi Dr. Chris, it's Ralph. I have a Charlie, here to see you. Shall I send him up?"

I pushed the button to speak back, "Please do, Ralph. Thank you!"

I had two minutes to pull my hair up into a bun and slide a bit of lip gloss over the curves of my lips before the elevator would get to my floor, and another 30 seconds to still my pulse and make it look like I hadn't been rushing around.

Knock, knock, knock, knock, knock I looked at my watch. It was 7:30 and he was at my door.

I peeked through the peephole and saw Charlie holding another light red carnation to the tip of his nose and looking back at me. I inhaled, took a second and opened the door.

"Good morning, Dr. Chris," he said, tipping the flower in my direction.

"Good morning, Charlie. Come on in. I just need to grab my boots and a coat."

I stepped to the side and ushered him inside, side hugging him before he could pass by completely.

He handed me the flower and I stuck it in the vase with the winter honeysuckle and turned raising an eyebrow in his direction before walking into the living room.

"I knew you wouldn't make it that easy for me to find the other carnation."

"Come on in, have a seat. Can I get you anything?"

"Nice place. No thank you, I'm okay."

"Okay, I'll be right back out with my boots." I dashed into the bedroom and came out with my winter duck boots.

He was gazing around at my condo when I came back into the living room. I sat down across from him on the sectional, and pulled my boots on.

"Did you find the place okay?"

"I did. Did you sleep well?"

"Maybe too well. I woke up about 15 minutes ago."

"You got ready that fast?" he asked with astonishment. I raised my arms to the side, shrugged my shoulders and tilted my head to the side. "Now I really am amazed."

"What's that?" I asked, lacing up the last boot.

"Nothing," he quipped with a smirk on his face that told me there was so much more that he was thinking.

He was wearing the red and white fair isle printed scarf I wrapped around his neck yesterday. So I reached over and tugged on it.

"Yeah, sorry. I didn't realize that I had it on until after I got off the phone with you. But I think it looks good though, don't you?"

"Sure does. Someone has good taste."

He snickered at my response and watched intently as I finished lacing up the last duck boot.

"Do you have everything you need?"

"I think I do. Are you ready to go?" I asked as I walked to the coat closet to grab my coat, hat, gloves and a scarf. He stood up from the couch and looked around the room.

"So where is the tree going?"

I looked around at the options. There were two, one by the window and one by the fireplace. I pointed them out to Charlie and decided on the spot by the window which meant that we would need to move a console table before we brought the tree in. That was the last thing we did before heading out for breakfast. We worked together to relocate the console table behind the sectional and did so without removing any of the decor resting on the top.

"Up top!" Charlie said, double high-fiving me after we successfully moved it without dropping anything. He looked at me as though he was impressed with my coordination. Without thinking, I flexed a muscle and motioned for him to follow me out.

I locked the door behind us and we headed towards the elevator. The doors opened instantly. I guess we were the only ones in the building that were up that early on this Sunday morning. I stepped in first, choosing a spot in the middle, as he placed his hand over the left elevator door so it wouldn't close on me. The doors closed behind him as he stepped inside and pushed L. He stood in the corner of the elevator and leaned up against both walls and looked in my direction.

"What are you doing way over there?" I asked him.

"Feeling vulnerable," he replied looking half-serious and half-playful.

"How so?" I asked him.

"I was thinking about everything I said to you last night and hoping that it didn't rub you the wrong way."

"I answered the door didn't I?"

"You did," he hesitated.

"But?"

"But then you side hugged me."

"Oh, sorry. I was in such a hurry this morning." Just as I was about to lean in for a proper greeting, the doors of the elevator opened.

Ralph was waiting for our exit, just as I assumed he would. "Good morning, Dr. Chris."

"Hey! Good morning, Ralph. You've met Charlie already this morning, right?"

"I have," he said.

"We're off to breakfast but we'll be back soon with a Christmas Tree."

"I'll have a cart waiting for you at the front desk."

"Much appreciated, Ralph," Charlie said.

"Yes, thank you," I echoed.

"Have a great morning."

Charlie reached down for my hand and squeezed it. "I was wondering how we were going to get a tree upstairs when I saw the path to your door."

I smiled before the door opened and the cold winds slapped me in the face.

"WOO! How close did you park, Charlie?" I asked before seeing his truck parked on the street, a few steps from the door.

He trotted to the truck, with me in tow and opened the door for me. "Are you in?" He closed the door after I nodded. Then ran around the front of the truck to get to his side.

"Are you sure we're getting a tree today?" I asked him.

"The lady requests a tree, we are getting," he started the engine, "a tree. But first, we eat."

He drove us to a small cafe that had vegan, vegetarian, and omnivore options. We ordered and ate by a street-side window when our food was ready. The food was delicious and we chatted about Christmas and Christmas-tree related memories.

"So Charlie, you're not from here. How did you find out about the Christmas Tree farm that you told me about last night?"

"I googled it since you called me on my landline. Is it okay?"

"That's the farm that my parents used to take my siblings and I to when we were in elementary school."

He almost spit out his coffee. "Are you kidding me?"

"I have lots of good memories there but I've never gone as an adult because I always vowed to go back when I started my own family."

His eyes were the size of saucers and he stared at me in shock.

"I picked the 3rd one on the list because the third time's a charm right?" I stopped to think about the number of times our paths had crossed and realized that in our scenario, it truly was. We met inadvertently at the coffee shop. Then I saw him the next day at the coffee shop from across the street, but we clicked after officially meeting at the hospital.

"You're right."

"Full transparency," he started and paused while finishing a bite of his turkey breakfast sandwich, "I almost called you this morning to see if we could postpone."

"What happened?"

"Yesterday was about as perfect a date as you could get. I didn't want to mess that up. I started thinking things could only go downhill from there."

I raised my eyebrows in disbelief.

"What changed your mind?"

He smiled, "I looked at that picture that you sent of the vase of flowers. There was a reflection of you in the print that was hanging above that table. The joy that was on your face is what changed my mind."

"Let me see that picture." He handed me his phone and told me that the password was his birthday. It was a test to see how strong my memory was. I closed my eyes and envisioned his face as he told me when and where he was born. I typed in 4 digits and the phone opened right up, which he somehow found funny. I navigated to the messages section and retrieved the message I had set last night. It took a few seconds to open, but there I was, cheesing as I took a picture of the honeysuckle.

"Do you see it?"

"I do. How did you see that?"

"It was meant for me to see so I could remember my why."

I looked down towards my sandwich, which was completely gone, and fiddled instead with the paper that held it before gazing out the window.

He placed his hand on top of my hand and tapped it lightly.

"Trust your gut Dr. Chris."

"I trust it, Charlie. Just trying not to get emotional so early on a Sunday morning."

"Maybe later today?" he chuckled.

"Maybe so."

We got all bundled up again and he helped me with my coat. I had chosen an older one so the sap wouldn't mess up one of my nicer coats. I forgot though, that the one I was wearing had a zipper that got stuck from time to time. This was unfortunately one of those moments. I struggled to get it to zip; yanking and pulling and nothing was moving. Charlie, without breaking eye contact, gingerly grabbed the zipper and slowly raised the pull, one tooth at a time until the coat was fastened.

"All good?"

"All good. Thank you."

"One more thing," he mentioned before grabbing my scarf from the booth and wrapping it around my neck, the same way I had protected his the day before. "You almost forgot your scarf," he said adjusting it until the sides were evenly draped.

"MmmHMM. Got it. Let's roll lady, we have a tree to find."

There I was speechless again. Meanwhile, that charming smile beamed across his face as he held the door of the cafe open for me. We hustled out to the pickup truck, attempting to dodge the wind's vicious 1, 2 combinations.

"Are you in?" he asked again before closing the door.

I was. I was all in, but he didn't know it. He hopped in the truck and looked over at me, with a face that said he was glad to see me sitting there. As though the gear shift was their cue, snow flurries started falling just as he placed the truck in drive.

"This looks like something from a movie," I told him. "All we need is some Christmas music and that's a wrap."

Charlie turned on the radio and switched it to a satellite radio holiday music station.

"Asked and answered," he joked.

I listened to the song that came on next and watched him as he drove us towards my first live Christmas tree in more than a decade. He started singing, "What are you doing, New Year's, New Year's Eve?"

I rested an open palm on the cup holders between us, which he promptly and proudly filled with his own hand. "Maybe I'm crazy to suppose, I'd ever be the one you chose..."

"Have you ever sung professionally

anywhere?" I was genuinely curious. His voice, slightly raspy but full of feeling, was beautiful and listening to him sing filled my soul with joy.

"Noooo. In fact, I haven't sang in front of anyone in a long time."

"Like how long?"

"Think 5th grade."

"Wow."

"Yeah, I told you that I held back pieces of me."

"Well, keep singing, please. I'm enjoying it."

"Only if you sing along."

"No sir, nobody wants that," I laughed.

"I do, but you have to answer my question first."

"What question?"

"What are you doing New Year's," he sang, "New Year's Eve?"

I squeezed his hand and listened to his voice

wrap its billowing words around my heart. The truth was that I had hoped for us to spend New Year's Eve together, but I didn't want to jinx anything.

"So, do you want the answer to that now or once we stop driving?"

"Tell me later. I'd like to maintain control of my driving senses."

"You bet. I'm sure this song will be the first one we hear again later on."

"I know it will."

We made our way to the tree farm and arrived just as they had opened for the day. They welcomed us in and gave us instructions for finding and cutting down the tree of our choice.

"How tall are your ceilings?" Charlie asked.

"11 feet, but how long is your pickup bed?"

"6 feet, but we can tie down whatever we need."

I asked for us to look at the 8-ft firs and we took off on foot, the snow wafting down around us. He carried the bow saw and I kept my eyes peeled for the perfect tree. It was just at the top of the hill, sitting on the crest, waiting for us to arrive and take it to its new home.

Charlie, handed me a pair of work gloves that he had picked up from the hardware store that morning. I held the tree while he was busy sawing it down.

"I think this tree needs a name," he offered.

Only two names came to mind, "Mortimer?"

He looked up at it curiously, "Definitely not a Mortimer."

"Randolph?"

"Yep. That's it. Watch your feet now. Randolph is about ready join the family."

"Whose family?" I asked, watching Charlie stop sawing just long enough to make eye contact with me and wink before returning to sawing and singing.

"Little Christmas Tree, no one to buy you, give yourself to me. You're worth your weight in precious gold, you see, My Little Christmas Tree. Promise you will be, nobody else's little Christmas Tree, I'll make you sparkle, just you wait and see. My little Christmas Tree."

I smiled at the sight of Charlie down on both knees, sawing and singing to the tree.

"With me you will go far. I'll show Saint Nick, the tree you really are. And there'll be peace on Earth when Daddy lights your star. My little Christmas Tree."

The tree snapped off just as he finished singing that stanza. And I started harmonizing the rest of the song with him.

"With me you will go far. I'll show Saint Nick, the tree you really are. And there'll be peace on earth when Daddy lights your star. My little Christmas Tree."

He turned and smiled at me, finishing the last line by himself. "You're big enough for three. My little Christmas tree."

I watched as Charlie grabbed Randolph, our 8.5 footer by the middle of its trunk and lifted it off the ground to shake out any possible critters that might have been hiding out. "Where did you learn that song, Charlie?"

He laid Randolph horizontal and motioned for me to grab the base of his trunk as he answered the question.

"My grandfather used to sing it every time we helped him decorate his tree. He never hung an ornament, but he always sang that song until we turned on the lights. He was the repeat button before there was a repeat button. You sounded good by the way!"

I giggled.

"Was this one of the songs that you sang with your grandmother?"

"It was. She used to play the notes of the bass clef on the piano while I would play the notes in the treble. That's how I learned to harmonize."

We walked Randolph back down the hill to the tree wrapping station where they shook the loose needles out and wrapped him up for easy transport. While they were loading him in the truck, I bought Charlie and I each a hot chocolate for the ride back into town.

One of the owners of the Christmas Tree farm had sent his daughter to take a few pictures of us in action. Instead she took a few short video clips of Charlie cutting down Randolph, then singing to it, me joining in, us walking it back to the barn and then some video of her brother taking a picture of us with the tree all loaded into the truck. He asked me if he could email the final montage to one of us once it was done, so I gave him my email address.

Charlie, hustled to my side of the truck to open the door for me. "Are you in?" he asked, then closed the door and away he went to hop in on his side. We rode in silence for the first few miles, watching to make sure that Randolph was well anchored down before turning on the radio again.

There she was again, Ella Fitzgerald singing, "What are you doing New Year's Eve."

"So your singing back there," I knew what was coming next, "was that the answer to my question?"

"What question?" I asked, feigning confusion.

"This question," he said, pointing to the stereo in his truck.

"Sure."

"I'm going to need more than that Dr. Chris."

"What else would help?" We were back in the city and just a block away from the condo, stopped at a red light.

"What are you doing New Year's Eve?"

"What are we doing New Year's Eve?" I asked him in return.

"Stethoscope," he said, acting like he was going to faint.

Ralph saw us pull up and rolled the cart out curbside for us, helping Charlie unload it from the truck. He asked if I would feel comfortable moving his truck and handed me the keys when I nodded in the affirmative. I told him to meet me on my floor and out I went, moving his pickup into the parking garage before hopping on the elevator, much to my surprise, with Charlie and Randolph. He explained that Ralph told him where to meet me.

"You tipped him well didn't you?"

"I'll never tell," he smiled.

We rode up to my floor in silence until he started humming, The Little Christmas Tree, again. We used the cart to roll Randolph to his new home in my condo. I grabbed the tree stand that I had bought last holiday season, but never used and brought it back into the living room.

The two of us worked to ensure Randolph was sitting as upright as possible before letting him rest for a while. Charlie took the cart back down to Ralph, and I placed my boots by the door so he would know to take his off when he came back inside.

I was in the kitchen cutting up onions and garlic for the chili when he came back upstairs. I offered him something to drink and snack on while he waited for the chili to be ready but had to point out where to find everything since my hands were full of onion and garlic oils. He offered to help prepare the meal, but I guided him to the location of the remote instead. He patiently waited on the couch and surfed through the tv for the pre-game shows. Once the onions and garlic had softened and the meat had been browned, I put the chili ingredients in the pressure cooker and let it do its thing. I quickly whipped up my ingredients for homemade cornbread and put that in the oven, before joining Charlie on the couch. I spent more time glancing over at Randolph than I thought I would.

It was the perfect space in the condo, in the perfect company, and Randolph really was my little Christmas tree. Charlie watched me admiring Randolph's empty branches and asked if we had time to decorate him before the game came on.

"Not quite," I told him with a bit of woe.

I sank closer to him on the couch and relaxed as he wrapped an arm around me.

"Thank you for Randolph."

"Of course, thank you for the experience."

I rested my head on the inside of his shoulder as he lightly caressed my arm, driving me straight to nap-town. At some point he must have grabbed the throw that was draped across the couch and instead let it fall onto the two of us. As I woke up to the sound of the pressure cooker timer, which startled both of us awake, I found myself tossing the throw aside.

Our bond was strengthened over the conversations we had while eating lunch. We cheered on the home team together while watching the game. Once it was evident that we had won, the two of us got to work decorating the rest of the condo, saving Randolph for last.

Ever the planner, Charlie turned on the tree decorating playlist that both he had created the night before. We strung the lights first, then draped garland and ribbons from Randolph's branches. "I feel like we're helping him get dressed," he chuckled.

"Just a few ornaments and we'll be just about finished!" I replied.

Thankfully we got to fill in the tree with the ornaments I didn't get to use last year. Once those were up, all we were missing was the star. I asked Charlie to place it atop Randolph's head before turning off the rest of the lights in the condo and asking the home assistant to turn on the Christmas Tree. There was at least peace in the condo as Charlie plugged the star into the rest of the lights.

He stood behind me, marveling at the tree while I glanced out at the city. There was peace out there too as a snowstorm pushed its way into the city limits, bringing nearly a foot of snow with it.

"Charlie, come to the window with me."

He looked out at the city then back at me with his mouth agape. I turned the tv back on just in time to see the local weather forecasters asking people to stay put where they were to prepare for the second round of this unexpected storm. We looked at each other and laughed.

"Looks like you're here for the night mister. Would you happen to have any comfy clothes in your truck?"

"Every self-respecting midwesterner carries an emergency bag with them during the cold weather months. I'll run down to my truck to grab it."

While I waited for him to return, I pulled an extra towel and wash cloth from the linen closet. It looked like we were about to have an unexpected nightcap.

Chapter 10
The Nightcap

Charlie:

I couldn't believe it. We were snowed in. I checked the weather before leaving the house this morning, but it didn't have anything to say about a winter storm that would drop a foot of snow, and the forecasters said it had circled back around to get us again. I had hoped that the two of us would have the chance to cross off some more of the list before this date was over, but it looked like that wouldn't happen until I remembered that we could add to the list. I was on my way back up to her condo after grabbing my emergency weather kit from my truck when I pulled out my cell phone and added two more items; get snowed in, and movie marathon with popcorn.

Dr. Chris' replies came in just as I stepped off

the elevators. "  "

I knocked on her door again then looked at my watch, it was exactly 12 hours after I had knocked this morning.

She had changed clothes completely in the few minutes I was gone and answered the door in sweatpants and a hoodie. She could not have looked more beautiful. Old Charlie would have held that inside. New Charlie had verbal diarrhea.

"Who is this beauty answering the door?"

She smiled a crooked smile, grabbed my hand and guided me inside, pulling me close for a hug.

"I owed you a better greeting, than the one you received this morning," she said, still locked in an embrace. She looked up into my eyes, and softly said, "I'm sorry you're stuck here."

"I'm not." It shot out of my mouth before I could stop it. She buried her head into my chest and I know she could feel my heart beating out of control. It pulsed like the drum beats that you hear on those nature shows. You know, the ones where a gazelle is trying to outrun a lion. It was wild kingdom in my rib cages, but I stood still, taking it all in - the smell of her hair, the placement of her hands, the way she felt in my arms.

This woman.

I held her for as long as she wanted, not moving, not shifting, just staying present until she released her clasp.

I set my cold bag down and took off my boots, placing them beside hers on the entryway tile just underneath the table that held the honeysuckle stems. She ushered me into the kitchen and ladled out a mug of hot cider for me and one for her. We sat down at the island across from one another and had an impromptu staring contest. I wanted to ask what she was thinking, but there was more mystery in not knowing. Without so much as a blink, she reached below the counter, pulled out a mason jar full of sugar plums, sat it on the counter like a boss, and slid it across to me. I was hype. She won. I lost my cool.

"Where did these come from?!"

"I made them."

"I mean, just like that? So laissez-faire? You made sugar plums and said it like that was normal. You are a wonder, woman."

She laughed so hard she snorted and reached for a spoon in embarrassment.

"What else do you do?" I asked, genuinely curious now that I had confirmed she was a marvel. I took a sip of the cider before she answered.

"A little bit of this, a little bit of that," she replied.

"What is in this cider?"

"Is something wrong with it?"

"No, it's better than the cider at our spot."

"We have a spot?"

"Don't we?"

She eyed me cautiously, as a sly smile graced her face, taking a sip from her mug of cider and choosing not to reply.

"What? Did I say something wrong?"

"No, Charlie." There it was. My name from her mouth.

Attempting to shift the focus off of my ears,

which I knew were about to turn red, I asked why she was looking at me like that.

"Just trying to figure you out," she said, still eyeing me over the top of her mug and hiding the rest of her face.

I took another sip of cider and held her gaze. It really was the best cider I've ever had.

"Are we eating more chili for dinner or would you like something else?" she asked.

"I'm open," I said, an ornery smile tipping the corner of my mouth.

She shook her head in reply and turned to open the doors on her french door refrigerator. I peeked in behind her to see how she stocked her fridge. It was full of veggies and fresh pressed juices, just as I had imagined.

I offered to prepare dinner for us and watched her slowly exhale through her lips before turning back to me and saying, "I'll gladly take you up on that, when we're at your place. When we're here though, let me take care of you."

I nodded at her, "Fair enough." I asked about her juicing and she lit up, telling me about the way juices restored her health at a time when she was eating poorly. She said she's never looked back which I admired. Speaking of which I still needed to find the carnation that she challenged me to find.

"So about this missing carnation..."

"You remembered."

"I did. How warm am I right now?"

"You're very cold," she replied, shaking her head.

I turned around and surveyed the room. I'd been here most of the day and hadn't found it yet. I also hadn't been to the gentleman's room yet either.

"Dr. Chris, could I use your bathroom?"

"Oh my goodness, I'm so sorry, Charlie. It's right down the hallway there."

I walked down the hallway and saw an extra towel and washcloth meticulously draped on the end of a bed in the first room on the left, which must have been the spare.

"Which door am I using, Dr. Chris?"

"Last door on the right."

I opened it, but I was looking at another bed and a nightstand that held the one single carnation in a clear glass bud vase. I closed the door quickly, assuming that was her bedroom. "On the right?"

"Sorry, no. Last door on the left!"

I opened the last door on the left to find the bathroom, which smelled just like the good doctor. I did what I had gone in there to do, washed my hands, and headed back towards Dr. Chris who had moved from the kitchen into the living room where she was gently touching Randolph's branches and humming The Little Christmas Tree to him. I stopped behind her, placing my hands on the outside of her shoulders, which triggered her head to follow me instead of the tree.

"So it's in your bedroom, eh?" I asked, raising both eyebrows in the center.

She smiled at me, "Admiration."

I laughed at the boomerang of my words. "So good doctor, how was I supposed to find that carnation without you sending me into the wrong room?"

A look of guilt spread across her face. "I had it on the fireplace mantle until you went downstairs to grab your bag."

I raised an eyebrow and slowly nodded at her answer. "Stop it," she replied seeming genuinely embarrassed that I'd had a glimpse into her bedroom.

I lightly squeezed her shoulders before walking over towards the window to see the snow. It was really coming down again. "Dr. Chris, this is bad." The snow drifts were so high, I could only see the tops of the trashcans, and the electrical boxes had snow halfway up their sides.

She moved to the window and wrapped her arms around me from behind. I held her hands with mine and leaned to the left so she could see what I was seeing.

"Ohhh!"

Dr. Chris:

We stood in silence and watched the snow fall from the heavens. It was a beautiful sight but I could see the strain on Charlie's face. I rubbed his back and asked if there was something else that was worrying him.

He hesitated. “No. This is just a lot of snow.”

“All the more reason to start this marathon of movies. Right?” I asked.

He nodded.

“I’ll get the popcorn ready.”

“Do you mind if I change while you’re doing that?”

“You can use the spare bedroom or the bathroom, both on the left. Whichever one you prefer.”

He grabbed his bag from the entryway and disappeared into the spare bedroom, returning a few moments later wearing a navy hoodie, and grey sweatpants. I almost burned the popcorn watching him walk to the island to grab his cider.

“What?” he asked with a smirk on his face.

“Stethoscope.”

He snickered and walked in the direction of the couch.

"So what movies are we watching tonight?" he asked, plopping down on the floor between the couch and the television.

"Whatever you'd like, sir."

I filled a big red bowl with the freshly popped popcorn and topped it with melted butter and a little bit of salt, tossing it high into the air to mix it all in. Charlie, turned and watched me while I was coating the popcorn.

"My mom used to mix popcorn like that," he said, with a boyish grin on his face.

"Oh yeah?"

"Mm hmm."

I reached into the fridge, pulled out two juices, and took them into the living room before returning to the kitchen to grab the bowl of popcorn and a couple of paper towels. As soon as I got back into the living room and sat on the couch, I sighed. I turned around to see the lights still on in the kitchen and Charlie quickly hustling in there to turn them off.

"I got it."

"Charlie, while you're up will you do me a

quick favor?"

He turned to face me with a grin, "Sure. What can I do for you?"

I looked at him, head cocked to the side, "Don't ask me that."

"What do you need, Dr. Chris?"

"In the hall closet, first door on the," I paused and held up my hands, dropping each thumb down to the side to see which formed an L, "on the right."

He opened the squeaky door.

"Will you choose one of those blankets for us?"

He pulled out a blanket that was a twin to the one we had used on our date, and brought it back to the couch. He raised it up to drape it over my legs and I slid in close to get comfy beside him. Feet propped up on the coffee table, I asked him if he would choose the first movie for us to watch. We alternated between our choices, all classics, laughing at the funny moments, reciting memorable lines together, me leaning in for comfort during the touching moments. We had watched 3 in totality and were in the middle of watching our 4th movie when the lights on Randolph dimmed then came back on.

I sprang to my feet, knowing exactly what was about to happen next. I only hoped that I could make it to the bag in the hall closet in time. No sooner than I opened the closet door did those lights go all the way out. Charlie grabbed his cell phone and turned on the flashlight, pointing it in my direction. I knocked the bag off the top shelf in the closet and from it grabbed two battery powered lanterns, turning them on and walking back towards the couch where Charlie was still seated. I placed one on the coffee table and helped him up off the couch, asking him to check the peephole to see if the hallway lights were out.

"Yep. Does that mean it's the building?"

I walked to the window and shook my head at what I saw. "It might be the block."

"I'll call to report the outage," he said in a very calm and matter of fact tone.

"I'm calling the hospital to let them know that the power is out here and that I'll keep them updated on whether or not I can get out of the parking garage tomorrow morning."

We ended our respective calls and I stepped closer to the window, feeling the chill being diffused from those floor-to-ceiling length panes of glass. With the city lights now muted by the power outage, the presence of the night stars became known. It was rare that I got to see those living in the city. I was taking in their beauty when I heard him.

"Come here, Dr. Chris," Charlie said with outstretched arms. I walked towards him with the second lantern which he relieved me of, placing it on the console table we had moved to its temporary home behind the couch earlier this morning. "Those windows are going to significantly cool this place down without any heat."

He held me for a moment then measuredly rubbed my arms and asked if I had a deck of cards. Grabbing his hand, I guided him back to the coffee table where I pulled a pack that would entertain us for the next two hours. The two of us sat on the floor, the blanket covering us from the waist down, playing go fish and old maid until it was too cold to do so anymore.

I stayed put while Charlie walked to the kitchen cabinet and grabbed a juice glass, placing it on the counter and his phone inside it to amplify the music he turned on. He extended one hand in my direction and methodically each finger folded towards his palm, motioning for me to join him.

The blanket fell as I stood up and the cold air spurred my legs into motion. I scurried to where he was standing and he held me like he had at the end of our date last night. That is, he held me like last night, before we were interrupted by Oakley's phone call. He started to sway to the beat of the music and before I knew it we were slow dancing all around the condo. We started rhythmically moving in the kitchen then a smooth transition took us near our tree Randolph, before finding us gracefully flowing into the living room. Eye to eye, the entire time. He used his hands to steady my balance and point me in the direction he wanted me to go.

Moving helped with the cold, but my nose was starting to feel a bit frigid and I told Charlie such. He stopped dancing long enough to get the blanket that I had left in a heap on the floor and used it to wrap us up like a stuffed crepe. I pulled his hood up over his head and quickly placed my hands between us for warmth, drawing each of them into a fist and up to my body like an x. I peered at his face, as he began to sway again. The lanterns had cast shadows upon us that seemed to make the situation dramatically more stirring. So coy, this one, as he gazed down upon me. I rested my head on his chest and heaved a deep sigh.

"Dr. Chris."

I pretended that I didn't hear him call my name. My fear was not that he would ask me why I sighed, but rather that I would tell him the truth.

"Dr. Chris," he said again.

"Yes, Charlie?"

A wistful look filled his face, "Where did you go?"

I searched for the answer in his eyes. My gut said it was okay to tell him, so I spoke methodically about how I was feeling. "Snow storm and power outage included," he increased the speed of our sway, "this day has been one I'll remember forever," *sway, sway, sway,* "for all of the right reasons." His swaying slowed again.

"And what would those reasons be?" he asked.

"Well there's really only one that matters," I said, speaking from my heart.

In any given moment we can choose when we tell the complete and unhindered truth and we can choose when we tell only part of it. So, while my gut told me it was okay to tell him that this was the day that "I knew," my head said tell him that you're enjoying his company.

"Tell me about that one then," he said. Because my arms were sandwiched between us, I could feel his heartbeat accelerate and strengthen with force.

"Remember two nights ago," swaying speed increased, "it almost feels like forever ago now," sway-sway-sway, "when we were on the phone and we were struggling to hang up?"

He moved, cheek-to-cheek, so I couldn't see his face anymore, which in theory should have made it easier to say what I was thinking. Instead I was transfixed by the feel of his facial hair on my cheek and chin.

"Mmhm" he tenderly replied.

"I feel like that right now," I finished.

There wasn't even a blink batted before his warm words tickled my ears, "I feel like that every time I'm near you." He lifted his head slightly and placed his forehead on mine, closing his eyes and touching the tip of my nose with his, pausing for a breath before continuing.

"I don't want this day to end, Dr. Chris. That's what I was thinking about when I was at the window earlier." I reached up and cupped his face with my hands, just as Marley had done to me, and inhaled deeply.

He started singing softly, "Promise you will be, nobody else's little Christmas Tree, I'll make you sparkle, just you wait and see. My little Christmas Tree."

And just like that, I melted.

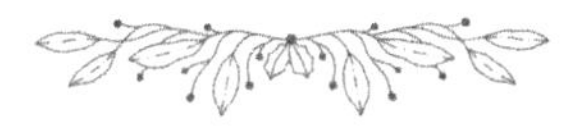

Charlie:

It was a moment that should have ended in a kiss, our first kiss. Instead it ended with a wedge driven between us. She had melted into my arms. I literally felt her weight shift as I was tilting my lips towards hers when the juice glass vibrated and we both glanced in its direction. There it was, a picture of Oakley on my screen. I hung my head and sighed. She broke from our embrace.

"I'll let you get that," Dr. Chris gracefully

replied as she left the living room and walked towards the bathroom. I know she was hot. That was twice now.

I silenced the call, not caring a bit about what Oakley had to say. I was done, done, as Steve put it, and it was nearly 11 o'clock at night. The only thing that call could be was bad. I had to block her number so she could stop blocking me. It was like she had a 6th sense or something! ARGH!!! I was so angry.

Dr. Chris returned from the bathroom quiet and looking as though she had a few words that she was stifling. I tried to cut the tension with laughter, but she read me the riot act with her eyes.

Finally, as she took a seat on the couch she spoke, "was she okay?"

"I don't know," I said, still standing.

"Why don't you know?" she asked.

I knelt in front of her, looked her in the eyes, palms up, heart open so she knew exactly how I felt. "I didn't answer the phone."

"Because...?" her words lingered in the air.

"Because I don't care what she wants. The only person I care about in this moment, right here is you."

She pursed her lips and nodded. I knew she wasn't okay but I didn't know how to fix it. Dr. Chris was battling something I had no control over. I just wished she would tell me what it was.

Either way you sliced it, it was still cold in the condo, so I covered her with the blanket we had been slow dancing in and sat down on the couch beside her, blowing warm air into my closed fists before tucking them into the pockets of my hoodie.

We sat in silence for a couple of minutes, her with a furrowed brow, and me contemplating all the ways in which I could cut off Oakley from my life.

"Hey Charlie," her words cut through the silence like a lifeline being tossed to a person lost at sea. I turned my head in her direction to hear her finish her statement. "It's still cold in here. Don't get sick." she said, opening the blanket for me.

There we sat. Me looking at her. Her looking at me. Us looking at each other with serious contemplation. The moment felt heavy. There was no other way to describe it.

"I'm trying, Charlie," she said. I could see tears beginning to flood her eyes so I reached for her hand and pulled her near, swinging my arm around to comfort her.

"Whatever it is, Dr. Chris, you can talk to me about it." I was so uneasy watching her cry. I felt helpless. It triggered a memory from childhood; a moment where I had found my mom crying. I felt helpless then too, but I wanted to fix it, whatever "it" was. My mom in her infinite wisdom, held my little chin and told me, "Sometimes son, you just have to let a woman cry. She'll let you know what she needs."

So I tried to apply that logic here, with Dr. Chris. I sat quietly and listened as she began to open up about the first man she trusted with her heart, and how he had dated someone else while he was dating her, all the while pretending like the woman who was calling him was something different to him than she was. I listened as she described how her gut told her one thing but she let her head lead her astray. I suddenly had more context for our prior conversation. She was battling discernment between her head and her heart.

"I'm sorry he hurt you in that way." It was the

only thing that crossed my mind to say.

She nodded and apologized for crying about it.

"Sometimes you have to just cry it out. Don't apologize for feeling. I'm just glad that you still do."

"What do you mean?"

"That you still feel. I'm glad you didn't let it crush your heart. That's what we do." The machismo thing again.

"Oh, my heart has been crushed several times over by the population I work with. Sometimes they survive and sometimes we hurt with their loss, right alongside their families. But that never stops me from investing in their wellbeing."

I nodded. Those were the words I needed to hear at the very moment I needed to hear them. What we were doing right now, what we had done yesterday, what we had done on the phone the night before that, was invest in each other's wellbeing. It wasn't about what we needed. I was more interested in taking care of her needs, and she had done the same for me. I was starting to understand more about Dr. Chris, and this conversation confirmed everything that my gut had been screaming at me.

I propped my feet up on the coffee table that still held the playing cards from our incomplete match of go fish, and she nestled in across my chest, her legs curled up on the couch beside me. I adjusted the blanket around her to make sure that everything was covered, and there we sat in silence, keeping each other warm, in body and soul. I tried my hardest to stay awake, but at some point our breathing synced and it hypnotized me right to sleep.

The last thoughts I recall were how cold my feet were and how comfortable I was with her in my arms. I know it had only been two days, but it felt like we had known each other for more like two decades. When I woke up, she was curled up in the same spot, resting peacefully as the sunlight began to peak through the windows and caress her face with its warmth. I stayed as still as I could and thought about my good fortune to walk into the coffee house at just the right moment.

This woman.

Chapter 11
Mr. & Mrs. Claus

The alarm on my phone woke me up. I had fallen asleep in his arms and wasn't sure what time it was. I bolted into the kitchen to grab my phone and stop the alarm. The power was still out and we were going on nearly 12 hours without it. I had 3 voicemail messages waiting for me so I stood at the island and listened, not wanting to disturb Charlie's slumber.

The first message was Marlo, checking to make sure I was safe during the power outages.

"Hey Chris. Heard you weren't sure if you were going to make it in today. Give me a call when you get the chance so I know you're good over there." *click*

The second voicemail was from the staff of

Hope Gardens, making sure I was safe.

"Hi Dr. Chris, we received your message and were checking in to see how you're doing. Keep us updated when you can." *click*

The last message was from Marlo again, asking if I could find a stand in for his role as Santa at tonight's Holiday Jubilee. "Hey Chris, it's me again. Hope you're doing better than I am. My car got stuck at the bottom of my street and has decided it's not moving. Unless there's a miracle, I'm not going to make it in to work today. I was hoping you KNEW someone who could stand in for me as Santa at the Jubilee. You know, someone, right? Give me a call to confirm. Thanks."

I dropped my head into my hands. I totally forgot that was today. I had to find a way to get there. I called the staff at Hope Gardens to see if they had enough people on shift today.

"We have enough to make it!" I was told.

"Is the Holiday Jubilee still on?"

"It is! We're so looking forward to the arrival of Santa Claus."

"So, funny story" I started. "I received a

voicemail from Marlo about 15 minutes ago. He's stuck at the bottom of his street and is waiting for a tow. He's not going to make it tonight and asked me if I could help him find a replacement Santa."

I could hear their disappointment from the other end. "We already told the children that Mrs. Claus might not be visiting, but that Santa would be there."

"Let me see what I can do," I offered before getting off the phone with them and glancing in Charlie's direction.

"Charlie?"

He yawned.

I stepped closer to him. "Charlie?" I called out, touching him on the shoulder. He grabbed my hand and kissed the back of it.

"Good Morning, Dr. Chris."

He awakened the butterflies in my stomach with that kiss. "Good Morning to you," I replied. "Did you sleep okay?"

"Mmhmm."

"Are you ready for breakfast?" I asked.

"Hey, listen," he said, scooting to the edge of the couch cushion. "Let me fix it for us. You made sure I had a warm place to stay last night."

I checked a light switch. The power was still off and it was a bit chilly in the condo.

"When we have power, you got me, right?"

"Totally forgot there's no power."

He looked confused. I had no intention of letting him cook anyway. The power outage was an easier way to let him down. "Your choices are cereal or oatmeal parfait, and juice or water."

"A parfait sounds so fancy," he said with intrigue written all over his face.

"Would you like one?"

"Yes, please, and a juice."

I quickly opened the refrigerator door to remove two fresh pressed juices and two oatmeal parfaits, closing the door just as quickly as I had opened it, in an attempt to keep as much cold air in as possible.

He pulled two spoons from the drawer and handed me one as he walked past me, returning to the seat where he ate chili yesterday afternoon.

We held hands across the island countertop as he blessed the food and I squeezed them with my "Amen," just as I had done throughout my childhood.

"Are we going to try to get you to the hospital today?" he asked.

I told him about the tradition behind the Holiday Jubilee, which had been started more than 50 years prior to ensure that the children who weren't able to be home for the holidays could still celebrate with their families. There were games, music, food, contests, the annual reading of "The Christmas Cookie," and always a visit from Santa and Mrs. Claus.

"But this year," I told him, "I was supposed to be Mrs. Claus, and Santa was supposed to be my friend, Marlo, who left a message for me this morning. His car got stuck in the snow and he was waiting for a tow."

His eyes lit up as he asked if he could fill in for Santa. He had no idea how happy I was to hear him volunteer in tribute. I didn't know how I was going to ask him to don a red suit, fake stomach, and further fill in his beard with grey hair. I think it must have been his desire to jump in and help that made me smile. We had a new mission for the day; get to Hope Gardens before the Jubilee. I sent text updates to Marlo so he could focus on his own mission - save the car.

We ate, and checked the weather forecast on our phones. Charlie excused himself from breakfast to step away into the bathroom and I moved our dishes into the sink with the rest of them that hadn't been washed last night. I moved to the best view of the city's road conditions, my big picture windows. The snow drifts were higher than they were when we looked last night. There were single lane paths that had been carved out by the snow plows, but nobody was traversing them. The buses didn't appear to be running. There weren't any pedestrians. The city appeared to be shut down, but that shouldn't stop the show.

Charlie joined me at the window and shook his head at the stillness of life outside the window.

"Are you sure you want to try it, Charlie? We could stay here if you think it's too dangerous."

"You were introduced to Chief yesterday weren't you?"

"Who's Chief?" I asked. I didn't remember meeting anyone with him yesterday.

"Chief carried Randolph home yesterday," he said with a smirk on his face.

"Ohh, your pickup truck."

"Yes! Chief and I have had several adventures together, including a road trip into the mountains of Colorado."

"Were the roads plowed?"

"Who said anything about roads?"

I couldn't tell if he was being serious or silly. His face read both so I just let it go. We agreed that we'd get cleaned up and make the trek out into the desolate and snow-packed streets of Kansas City to drive the 5 miles to Hope Gardens.

"We have to at least try," he insisted, and try we did. We rotated turns in the bathroom getting cleaned up, and we repacked Charlie's cold weather bag before grabbing our coats, boots and heading out for the day.

We made our way down to the parking garage via the stairs. It wasn't bad on the way down, but

I was hoping for the power to be restored once I got back here. Living on one of the highest floors normally had its perks, but this was one time when I would have preferred to live on any floor below the 10th.

Charlie unlocked the doors of his truck and opened the passenger door for me, helping me inside. "Are you in?" he asked before awaiting my confirmation, closing the door and walking towards his side of the truck. He paused for a second and snapped his fingers like an idea struck him, before asking me to pop the trunk on my vehicle so he could grab the emergency bag out of my car, as he put it, "so we have double what we need, just in case." I obliged and he placed the bag in the rear passenger section of his quad cab before getting inside. Better safe than sorry always works for me, though in some matters it does more damage than good. That was in matters of the heart though, but not in practical matters like sledding through the streets of Kansas City in a pickup truck.

"Are we ready?" he asked. I double-checked my seat belt and he double-checked his own. I nodded in the affirmative and he looked for any oncoming cars before pulling out of the parking spot. I guided him through the turns of the garage towards the correct exit and once the doors opened, we were met with a near blinding amount of snow. From down on the ground it looked much worse than it did from above. There were miles of vehicles locked in on the side of the roads by the plowed snow. Some of them looked like they had gotten stuck, while others looked like they had parked in those spots intentionally.

Chief handled the snow like a champ on the flat roads. But I was admittedly nervous as we approached the hills of the city. If we hit just one patch of poorly located ice, there was nothing we could do. Charlie geared down as we slowly ascended the first hill. Slow and steady, right? He was stoic as Chief crested the hill and the engine roared on the way down. Only a slight tailspin as we bottomed out, but that was nothing compared to what awaited us around the corner. As Charlie made the right hand turn towards the hospital, he had to slam on the brakes, which sent Chief into a 360 degree spin. Charlie's arms went into overtime, cutting the steering wheel to the left, and the right, then back to the left before throwing the gear into park bringing the truck to a full stop. I'm still not sure how he was able to stop it without hitting anything, but we successfully avoided turning a 5 car pile-up into a 6 car pile-up.

"Are you okay?" he asked.

"I'm fine, Charlie. Are YOU okay?"

"I think so. That was a bit too close for comfort though."

"Are you sure, you're okay?"

"I think my life flashed in front of my eyes, as I was steering us out of the way."

I just listened, not knowing what to say.

He looked over at me and smiled. "I think I caught a glimpse of the future too." He shook his head in dismay thinking about it, then gasped with fright after he caught a reflection of another car barreling towards us in the side view mirror. "HOLD ON!" he shouted as he grabbed my hand and leaned me away from the door. The car coming from behind passed within an inch of us, becoming the 6th car in that pile-up.

"Now THAT was too close. Can you get us out of here?" I was extremely nervous. So much so that my hands were trembling.

Charlie checked the mirrors for any additional vehicles before placing Chief in off-road mode and slowly driving out of the mess with two tires trekking up on the piles left by the snow plows.

"Chief you're the real MVP," I said petting the dash board of Charlie's truck as we cleared the massive accident and rolled towards the refuge of the hospital. I glanced over at Charlie, whose chest puffed with pride at the ability to protect me with his pickup truck. He quickly returned the glance, winking my way before returning his eyes to the road. Just a couple of turns later we were pulling into the staff parking lot at the hospital. The security guard, stopped us, not seeing a parking pass and not recognizing Charlie or his truck, so we rolled down the window so I could wave.

"Dr. Chris! You made it!"

"Hi Jake, I did thanks to Charlie and Chief," I said pointing to each respectively.

"Here's a temporary pass for you, Chief," said Jake sliding the pass onto the dash of the truck before turning to greet my driver. "Nice to meet you, Charlie. That's some precious cargo you've got there."

"Likewise, Jake." Charlie said extending his hand through the window. "She is pretty precious. Glad we made it here safely."

Jake chuckled, and the two of us locked hands out of his sight and rolled into the lot.

"So here's the thing, Charlie," I started. "This is the first time I've ever brought anybody here to the hospital with me." Suddenly I was nervous. "People will have comments and questions, I already know."

"So what's our back story?"

"No back story, we tell them the truth."

A smile tipped the corner of his mouth and his eyebrows raised in surprise, "The truth?"

I wondered the same thing after I heard the words escape my mouth. "Yep. The truth."

"And if they ask about our relationship, I tell them..."

I paused to think about what I wanted him to say and I decided that it didn't matter what I wanted. He had a say in this too. "You tell them whatever you feel about our relationship."

"So I tell them that you're my little Christmas tree?"

I chuckled and asked him, "Is that what you want to tell them?"

"Well, as long as that works for you." We

were stuck. I didn't want to put any words into his mouth and he didn't want to put any words in mine.

"If you were to call your mom and tell her about me, what would you say?"

"Uhh...I can't tell you that," he said getting out of the truck and running over to my door before I opened it myself.

He opened the door and I grabbed his hand and hopped out. "Can't tell me? I thought you were being open and honest with me."

"Patient-client confidentiality?" he asked while wrapping an arm around me and closing the truck door. "Let's go Mrs. -"

"Stethoscope."

"Claus. Mrs. Claus. What were you thinking ma'am?"

Nothing. I wasn't thinking anything. But my heart felt that Mrs. in a manner completely different than he had intended. I let it go and walked into Hope Gardens with Santa Claus.

We greeted the staff on our floor and were briefed on the plan for the Holiday Jubilee. The two of us were ushered into one room where the costumes greeted us. Charlie's breathing became more rapid as he inhaled and scratched the back of his head.

"So," he cleared his throat, "you can go ahead and change first and I'll guard the room." Charlie was flustered at the thought of the two of us getting in costume in the same location.

"Charlie, there's a privacy curtain here and a bathroom with a door, right over there if you need it."

"Got it," he said while staring me down and sliding the privacy curtain across its track eventually eclipsing his face.

"Charlie?" I started.

"Santa," he responded.

"Santa?" I began again.

"Yes, Mrs. Claus?"

"You forgot your Santa Suit," I said, handing the suit to him from my side of the curtain.

I had the tendency to change pretty fast, so as I was pulling up my knickers and zipping up the dress, Charlie was still trying to figure out how to put on Santa's belly.

"Hey, Santa."

"Yes ma'am?"

"How are you doing over there?"

"I'm getting by, Mrs. Claus. How about you?"

"Almost done husband," I said while he chuckled aloud.

"Ho! Ho! Ho!" He changed into his character voice, "Mrs. Claus?"

"Yes, Santa?" I answered.

"Does, Mrs. Claus have a first name?" he asked me.

"Anya."

"That's right. Santa Claus the Movie."

"You remember that?" I asked, amazed that anyone other than me remembered that movie.

"Ho! Ho! Hooooo!"

"Oh, Santa. Are you dressed yet over there?"

"Santa may need a little help, Anya."

"Are your pants on, Santa?"

He completely broke character. "Yes, my pants are on Dr. Chris!"

Through laughter I spoke, "I'm moving the curtain." I pulled the curtain back and chuckled at the sight of Charlie in his belly suit. I helped him put on and buckle the belt over his coat, and while he was putting on his boots, I colored his beard and hair silver. He put on his hat and looked in the mirror.

"Get out of here!" he tilted his head from side to side, checking out my beard transformation. "I really look like Santa."

"You are Santa." I fixed his collar and brushed the velvety texture of his coat.

He placed his hands on my hips and slid back into character, "You look beautiful, Anya."

"Thank you, Santa."

"Oh ho ho, of course dear. How long have we been married now?"

"I think it's been more than 200 years."

"I see. I see. Well that explains why I have a hard time remembering just how long."

"The children are waiting to see you, Santa."

"Children? We have children?"

"The children of Hope Gardens, Santa."

"Oh, right. So silly of me. I must have slipped out of character." He popped his eyebrows at me when I realized that I didn't add any grey to those. I did a quick touch up as he waited patiently, smiling at how serious I was about those eyebrows. Just as I was finishing up the details of his final brow, in steps our administrative assistant, Susan, who today was dressed as an elf, checking to see if we were ready to go. I handed Charlie his fake spectacles and smiled at this man who had transformed his total being into Santa Claus to support the children of this hospital.

"Do I look okay?" he asked while spinning around in a circle. Susan and I looked at each other, then back at Santa Charlie, before nodding in union.

Susan gave us one final briefing on our tasks,

"It should only be about an hour, but if you get too hot or need something, come find me."

Santa grabbed my hand and off we went down the hallway for our grand entrance into the cafeteria. The music was pumping over the PA system and the children were in the middle of a dance party. Just before we entered, the DJ dimmed the lights, ducked the music, and announced, "Kids, I think we have some special visitors here all the way from the North Pole! Are you ready to see them?"

The children looked at their parents with shock and squealed, leaving the DJ hanging. So he asked again, "Are you ready to see them?"

The children shouted in unison, "Yes!"

The DJ replied, "If you're ready to see our guests let me hear you make some noise!!!"

The joy that abounded from their shouts is something I won't soon forget. I squeezed Charlie's hand, suddenly feeling nervous about playing Mrs. Claus. He looked over at me with a reassuring smile and nod.

From the DJ came a call and response that had the entire cafeteria, parents too, rocking for Santa and his wife. Then with a funky rendition of Little Drummer Boy ushering us in, the doors were opened by two elves and before I knew it, Charlie had grabbed my hand and danced us into the cafeteria with the kids, who jumped up and down like they were in some sort of candy cane rave. The two of us had our first dance with each other, then with each subsequent song the DJ invited the children, some of their family members, and eventually some of the elves to join in as well. Before I knew it we were all doing a Christmas remix of the Cha Cha Slide, after which Anya needed to take a break. I was worn out, but the DJ kept the party going for all who wanted to dance.

I stepped away to play some board games with those who were not interested in the dance party. We had the chance to chat about what their wishes were for the coming year.

I took notes on a pad of paper and told them that I'd pass along their thoughts to Santa.

Santa tagged me in for the dance party and swapped spots with me to catch a bit of a break. I saw him slip out of the cafeteria for a moment and then slide back in about ten minutes later. The children were so busy dancing that they didn't seem to notice he was gone. Much to my surprise, Santa gave the DJ a break and started spinning some tunes for a bit as the parents pulled out their phones and started recording. I looked at Charlie - Santa, wondering what other talents he was hiding inside. He was legit. Just as the DJ returned, Santa whispered something in his ear and hopped out of the booth, headed in my direction. The song that was on wound to a close and the DJ hopped back on the mic with another announcement.

"Alright parents, grab your children for our final dance of the night. We're gonna slow this one down a bit because we heard it's almost bed time." The DJ looked at me and smiled, "We have a very special dedication for this one. This song goes out to Mrs. Anya Claus and Randolph the tree, from Santa Claus."

Up rolls the music, from jazz master, Nat King Cole and his Trio. "Little Christmas Tree, no one to buy you, give yourself to me, you're worth your weight in precious gold you see, my little Christmas tree."

Santa grabbed my hand and we slow danced around the cafeteria stopping by each child and their family, wishing them all a good night and Happy Holidays before dancing back to the center of the makeshift dance floor for one final dip. Was Charlie a ballroom dancer in a different career? He made my clumsy two left feet appear to be in good working order.

We waved goodbye to all of the families, then hand-in-hand, made a dash through the double-doors of the cafeteria.

We stayed in character all the way down the hallway as some of the children were already on their way back to their rooms. Once we found our elf, Susan, she took us back to the door they had decorated to look like a Top Secret exit. Charlie was all smiles as we got back to the room.

"Do you think I can do this next year?" he asked me.

"I'm sure I can arrange for you to do that." I didn't know if he was including me in that with him or if it was just for him.

"I meant us, Anya. You were a great wife." Well there was my answer.

I shook my head and closed the curtain so I could quickly change in privacy.

"Charlie, thank you for helping me with this. You must be exhausted." There was silence. No reply, then all of the sudden I heard him let out an exhasperated sigh.

"Anya, I think I'm stuck."

I chuckled at the thought of him wrestling with that outfit. "Anya is gone, Santa."

"My wife is gone?"

"She is, but I can help you."

"Dr. Chris, unless I'm driving home in this, I know I'm going to need your help."

"Can I move the curtain?"

"You can. I have pants on."

Charlie was stuck in the belly suit. He couldn't get it back over his head, so I lifted it up as high as I could for him to wriggle out through the bottom. I handed him the suit and closed the privacy curtain once more.

He finished changing and moved the curtain back. He was dressed in his normal clothes but his beard and hair were still grey, making him look like a distinguished gentleman.

"Are you ready to go?" he asked me, eyes still full of life.

"We're supposed to wait in here until they get all of the families in their rooms," I told him. So we waited and I asked about his DJ skills. As it turns out, Charlie used to be a DJ in college, but only pursued it as a hobby in his spare time after graduation. He told me all about how he used to DJ in a nightclub on the weekends and his goal was to get everybody out of their seats. That definitely happened at the Holiday Jubilee. Even those who weren't dancing early during the celebration found their way to the dance floor while he was on the wheels.

I don't know which I was more impressed by, his DJ skills or his dancing skills. I had already received a preview of them yesterday while we were trying to stay warm in my condo, but I certainly wasn't expecting to be dipped at the end of the celebration today. I wanted to ask where he learned to waltz like that. But that question would have to wait. Just as I was about to ask it, in walked Susan, not the elf, but regularly dressed Susan, to let us know that all of the children were back in their beds and the hospital was in lights out mode.

We walked out with Susan prepared to head to the truck but instead were greeted by the hospital staff clapping and cheering on our appearance as Santa and Anya. They asked where I'd found Charlie, and thought he was the perfect Santa.

"So Charlie, how do you know Dr. Chris?"

Susan asked him trying to squeeze out as many details as she could.

"We actually just met a couple of days ago," he said "and I've been following her around ever since." They all laughed, but the truth is, that he wasn't that far off.

"No really, how long have the two of you been together, Dr. Chris? You two moved like you know each others thoughts," an orderly asked.

"So, I bumped into him a little bit more than a week ago and we had our first date on Saturday," it was the truth. That's what we decided to stick to.

"We don't believe you. There's no way!" they all chimed in.

We shrugged. "You don't have to believe us if you don't want to," Charlie said with a belly laugh that resembled that of Santa. "Okay folks, I have to get Mrs. Claus back home," he joked.

"We'll see you soon, right Santa?"

He nodded as I told the staff that I would see them tomorrow. He slid his arm around my shoulders and I heard them "aww" as we walked down the hallway towards the elevator.

This was new. All of it. Me sharing my work life with someone else. The staff seeing me do so. Me sharing my personal life with someone else. It's not something I saw coming at all, but it was something that at this moment I actively wanted to continue. I had a full life without him, but this was an extra bonus, that so far I was enjoying.

Charlie had a penchant for taking care of me and I had to admit it was nice to have someone other than friends and family care for you in this manner. As the elevator doors closed, I found myself lost in my thoughts, while he simultaneously attempted to get my attention. It took a slight nudge to my arm for me to come back from my flight of fancy before I glanced up at Charlie, who was holding back his charming smile and a laugh. I tried to read his thoughts again, but was still fighting to suppress my daydreams which drifted slightly again thanks to those eyes. They darted up to the ceiling of the elevator and back to my face. I followed his glance upwards to see that someone had hung a sprig of mistletoe from the ceiling and we were standing directly underneath it.

Not a word was spoken as I returned my gaze to Charlie's hickory brown eyes. I could feel his hands firmly on the small of my back. He gently pulled me in closer, using them to guide me in the same manner as he had when we were out on the dance floor. My body listened to his, and before I knew it, my arms were wrapped around his back, placing us chest to chest in an embrace that I knew in my gut was about to change my life. An acoustic guitar purred, "Have Yourself a Merry Little Christmas," throughout the elevator, and the scent of his body wash embedded itself on my memory banks. He lowered his cheek to mine and we swayed with the music until the guitar slowed, spurring Charlie into action. He leaned in and discreetly placed his lips on mine in a fiery embrace that took my breath away. Without so much as a word, his lips told me everything that he was thinking, and my soul heard all of it. Just as the guitar told us for the final time to have ourselves a merry little Christmas, the elevator doors opened, halting our kiss but not the encircling of our hearts.

He spoke softly, uttering only one word before we headed to his pickup truck and out into the night, "Stethoscope."

Chapter 12
Hot Cider

Charlie:

I found her, or she found me. Maybe we found each other. Either way, I was grateful for our chance encounter at The Fresh Grind. It led me here, to a place where I was still floating on a cloud after our impromptu date at the hospital. We had danced the night away in our mythical coupledom and I saw the side of her that Steve had tried to convince me was special. I watched her as she was dancing and chatting with the children, and each of them she treated as though they were the most special person in the world. My admiration increased ten-fold as I got to be the proverbial fly on the wall that night. And I don't have to tell you how eternally grateful I am to the person who left the mistletoe in the elevator. The feel of her lips lingered on mine long after I dropped her off at the condo.

I walked her upstairs, to ensure that the power had been restored and that all was well before I left for the night. I was open to wherever this journey took us, and though I had hopes of what that path might include, I was still nervous at the thought of being that vulnerable with someone again. The last time that happened, well, we don't need to talk about Oakley anymore. That's a done deal, or at least it was about to be a done deal.

Leaving Dr. Chris' condo, was the first time I had glanced at my phone since putting it on silent after last night's interruption. In addition to a missed call from my mom, I had 3 missed calls from Oakley and voicemails that accompanied each of them. I didn't know what she wanted, but I knew better than to listen to those while I was still in this building. So from my truck, I listened to each of her messages, confessing how she felt about me and some nonsense about seeing me for the gem that I was. She was not about to ruin this for me, and I had to tell her that in person.

By the time I got back to my house, I had decided that tomorrow I needed to stop by the Fresh Grind, so I could help her understand that I had no desire to be with her. In the meantime, there were two calls that I needed to make.

"Hi, Mom!" I said, excited to hear her voice.

"Oooooh, who is she Charlie?"

"Who is who?"

"Don't you make me ask again, son. I can hear it in your voice."

I cleared my throat. "Hear what, ma?" I said, fruitlessly trying to shift the tone of my voice.

"Charles Lane Hughes, what is her name? You can't fool your mother, dear." She was right and I knew it. Plus, I knew I didn't have a choice but to speak up. She used all three names.

"I don't know if I'm ready to tell you yet, mom."

"I can hear your smile through the phone, so I know she makes you happy."

"She does."

"Is she kind?"

"Yes ma'am."

"Is she caring?"

"Yes ma'am."

"Is she considerate?"

"Yes ma'am," I said, helping mom to understand that she met the trifecta that she had encouraged me to search for in a partner.

"What's her name, Charlie?"

"Chris."

"You take care of her, and I guarantee if she's kind, caring, and considerate, she'll do the same for you, Charlie."

"I will mom."

"So, I saw that there was a lot of snow there. Are you okay?"

"I am. I'm just getting home now." I probably should have changed the subject instead of answering this one honestly but I can't lie to my momma. She could be 1500 miles away from me and she'd still know I wasn't telling the truth.

"Just getting home?" she asked.

I tried to rush through my explanation as though it were no big deal. "I got accidentally snowed in at Dr. Chris'. Don't worry, I was a gentleman. I slept on the couch." Mom didn't need to know that she had too. “Today I helped her drive into work at the children’s hospital.”

“She works at a Children’s Hospital?” Mom’s interest was piqued.

“Yes ma’am. She’s a doctor. Anyway, I got her to work safely, stayed to play Santa for their holiday party for the children, and then took her back to her place to make sure that the power was back on before coming back here, to my house.” I thought I had been super nonchalant about everything, until Mom spoke up.

“You love her.”

“Ma!”

“I can hear it in your voice.”

“Okay, mom, I gotta go make sure my house is good.”

“Are you coming home for Christmas this year?” she asked, changing the subject.

“I don’t know yet. Can I let you know in a couple of days?” I truly didn’t know, but I was grateful for options.

“We only have a couple of days before

Christmas, Charlie."

"I know, mom."

"You can bring Chris with you if you want to." She hadn't changed the subject at all.

"Okay, mom, I gotta go. I'll call you soon okay? I love you!"

"Love you both!" she joked before hanging up the phone.

I hopped out of the truck and inspected the exterior of my house before going inside. For whatever reason, we didn't seem to have as much snow as they had received downtown, which was a relief to me. The house was in good shape, but was I? I still had one phone call to make.

I sat down on the couch to brace myself for this one.

"Hi Charlie!" her voice chirped as she answered the phone.

"I know I haven't been gone for that long, but I've missed your voice, Anya."

"The feeling is mutual, Santa," she said with

a chuckle that made my heart skip.

"Did you make it home safely?" she asked.

"I did and I have to tell you. It just doesn't feel as festive here." *So much honesty. Was that too much?*

"Do I need to come and help you decorate over there?" she asked. *Not too much honesty.* I breathed a sigh of relief.

"That would be great, but I don't think it's the decorations that would make a difference."

"Oh, what else would you need?"

"I think you know, Dr. Chris."

Her voice softened, "Charlie."

"Yes?" My pessimistic side was on the take over. I thought she was about to tell me that she wanted out.

She spoke two simple words that erased my cynicism, "I know."

"What do you know?" I asked, seeking clarification before getting overly excited.

"I *KNOW*." There was so much emphasis placed on the know. My heart smiled.

"Yeah, me too." We sat in silence, understanding that we were acknowledging a mutual feeling in the depths of our soul that affixed us for the foreseeable future.

"Does it seem fast to you?" she asked me.

"It does, but I don't doubt a second of it," I told her. "This is just different. I can't explain it. It's a - a truth, a knowing, that's always been a part of me, but in a space that I hadn't yet discovered."

"Same."

"I didn't know what to do with it until the elevator and the -"

"Mistletoe?"

"Mistletoe, yes." I was relieved to know that she felt what I felt and was anxious to see her again. "So you work tomorrow, right?"

"I do, but during regular hours. I didn't pick up an extra shift."

"Tomorrow evening, Steve and Sabrina host their annual Holiday Party. It's always on the

23rd. Would you like to join me?"

"I'd be honored to, Charlie." *This woman.*

"Great, I can pick you up again, if that works."

"It does."

"So I'll text you tomorrow with a pickup time. Is that okay with you?"

"Sounds perfect."

"Okay, Dr. Chris. You have a good night."

"You too, Charlie."

"Sleep well, beautiful."

"You too."

I hung up the phone reassured that I was marching into the same future that I had envisioned when we nearly got into that accident today. There was just one thing that needed to be resolved. So tomorrow, was the day that I fully stepped into that future.

I fell asleep with visions of Anya Claus, dancing in my head and woke up to a text from her, wishing me a great day.

I replied, "Looking forward to seeing you tonight."

I had lots of tasks to accomplish in a short period of time today. I needed to get our white elephant gifts for tonight, plus pick up a special Christmas gift for Dr. Chris, before going to set the record straight with Oakley. I grabbed my phone and set up tasks for the day to keep me on schedule, then got cleaned up so I could get a move on.

The first two were quickly knocked off the list, but I found myself dreading the last one. If I didn't do it, she would continue to call me, or worse yet, make a scene when she finally saw me. And let's be clear, in Kansas City, she would've seen me again, likely with Dr. Chris. So, during the lunch hour, I decided it was time to go grab another hot cider.

I hopped in the pickup truck and headed towards the Fresh Grind, with thoughts of the last few days with Dr. Chris, filling my head. Once I had arrived at the coffeeshop, I was firm in my resolve to walk inside, which is exactly what I did.

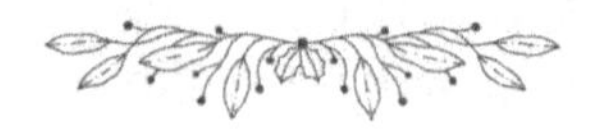

Dr. Chris:

I had grabbed lunch with Marlo at our usual spot so I could catch him up on all that he had missed; the first and second dates, the nightcap, the Holiday Jubilee. He had missed so much in a short period of time, and I had a lot to tell him.

"So, you kissed him on the elevator that we take upstairs to work everyday?" he asked putting on a false display of shock.

"I know," I told him.

"Did you see it when you got in the elevator today?"

"No, I felt it when I got in the elevator today."

"That must have been some kiss," he said, grinning like a Cheshire cat.

"Yep." There were so many more words I could have used, but yep held all of them in one tiny package that said don't ask me anymore questions about the kiss.

"So when are you going to see him again?" Marlo asked.

"Tonight," I said smiling.

"I love to see you so happy, Chris! Out of all the guys we've talked about - "

Unwilling to go down that path with Marlo right now, I changed the subject. "So you've been in and out. What's going on with you?"

"Don't tell anyone else at work, but I completed the final interview for that position at the Children's Hospital in Colorado. I'm supposed to find out about it before Christmas."

"I love it! You better keep me updated!"

"You know it."

We finished up our lunch conversation and I suddenly had a desire to grab a hot cider from across the street. I invited Marlo to join me, but he passed. So I told him that I'd meet him back at the office and hopped across the street to the Fresh Grind.

I heard his voice as soon as I walked in the door. He was sitting with Oakley again and though I wasn't trying to eavesdrop, I couldn't help but hear their conversation.

She leaned in closer to him, "I love you, Charlie."

He replied, "Oakley, there will always be a place in my heart that belongs to you."

I left, not wanting to hear anymore. Maybe I wasn't willing to hear anymore of it. The phone calls weren't accidental. They were intentional. She still wanted him. I could see it in her eyes, in the way she leaned in to talk to him, the way she reached for him as I was leaving. I couldn't will myself to stand in their way, no matter how much I thought I knew. It was just like the first time around. That was the point that I began to question everything that I had experienced over the weekend. I couldn't decipher whether I had trusted my brain or my heart. I didn't know how to tell the difference. I just knew that I couldn't possibly see him this evening. I couldn't pretend that I hadn't heard what I heard. I couldn't pretend that I didn't see what I just saw.

I went back to work and couldn't find Marlo. So, having nobody to process this one with, when they asked me about picking up another shift at work, I accepted. When Charlie sent me a text, just as he promised, I let him down as easily as I could - texting him back that I had taken on another shift.

"Can I bring you anything?" he offered.

"I picked up some extra food and cider

during lunch today."

"Can I call you later?" he replied.

"No worries. Call you after the holidays," I typed.

I didn't have any desire to see him again before Christmas, and all that New Year's Eve stuff, well I had to put that out of my mind too.

All of this because I decided that I wanted some hot cider.

Chapter 13
Steve & Sabrina's Party

Charlie:

I was completely confused as to what had happened. That morning I called Steve to let him know that Dr. Chris was going to be my plus one for the evening and he was so excited that he put me on speakerphone so Sabrina could also hear about our date or dates. They were both eager for her to be joining the festivities that evening and I was too.

I told them that I knew, that she knew and both of them congratulated me on finding her.

"So when did you actually meet her Charlie?" Sabrina asked me again.

"Do you remember when I bumped into the

mystery woman at Oakley's coffeehouse?"

"Yes," she replied.

"NO!" Steve shouted.

"Yep!" I confirmed. "She was the mystery woman."

"Get outta here," Sabrina laughed.

"The Universe was looking out for us," I told them. "When she walked into Jax's appointment, I just about lost it."

"There was no just about, Charlie," Sabrina shared. "You stood up the entire time, stammering over your words."

We all laughed.

"Sabrina Effect," Steve said.

"I knew you'd met her before when she called you Charlie," Sabrina said.

The two of them were looking forward to hosting this year, and I was looking forward to sharing my friends with Dr. Chris. I told them that I was on my way to see Oakley, to confirm that there wasn't a chance for her to be in my life anymore, not as a friend and certainly not as more than that. They both thought that it was a good idea, but asked if I had told Dr. Chris that I was on my way to do so.

"It'll only take me a minute," I told them.

Steve told me it was a bad idea. I should have listened but I thought I knew her better than they did. *Machismo.*

I visited the Fresh Grind and asked Oakley if she could join me for a few minutes. She happily obliged, not knowing what was on the way.

"I need you to know that I've found the woman I'm going to spend the rest of my life with," I started before she interrupted me, completely misunderstanding the words I had just spoken.

"I love you, Charlie," she said to me. I didn't feel a single thing and that made me smile.

"Oakley, there will always be a place in my heart that belongs to you," I told her before continuing, "but that place is small and shared amongst those people who I used to have a connection with."

Oakley's face was crestfallen. It looked like she had suddenly lost a dream that filled the innermost parts of her mind for the last year.

I continued, "There was a moment when I thought you and I would grow old together. There was a time when I told myself that you were the one, but that all came from a place in my head and not my heart. I know now that there's a difference."

"She's a lucky woman, Charlie."

"I'm a lucky man, Oak." I believed that with my whole heart. "But I didn't find her until I let go of you, and you have someone amazing out there waiting for you."

She smiled at me. "But I have to let go of you first."

"You do. Yes," I confirmed. Oakley nodded in acknowledgement of her need to let the past remain just that.

A hint of a smile started to peek through her melancholy face, "Charlie, go get her."

"You already know, I am." I could hardly wait to end this conversation, so I could go get her. "All the best, Oakley," I said as I hopped up from the table and dashed out to Chief on the way to the florist to pick up some flowers for my lady.

Having that conversation with Oakley was like a ten pound weight being lifted off my shoulders. I was free to explain to Dr. Chris that I had, in no uncertain terms, communicated my intentions with her, to Oakley. I couldn't wait to tell her so there weren't anymore lingering questions.

I sent her a text to see how her day was going and check in for tonight.

"I'm sorry Charlie." My heart sank after her reply popped up on my screen. "They asked if I could cover another shift tonight and I accepted."

Knowing that an extra shift would make for a very long day, I asked if there was anything she needed. She declined, sharing something about getting extra food and cider at lunch. I wondered if she'd seen me with Oakley and I asked if I could call her later - hoping that it would give me the chance to see what was going on.

Her reply was still rattling around in my brain. It felt like a dagger to my heart. She would catch up with me after the holidays. Did that include Christmas and New Year's Eve? I didn't know what it was, but something wasn't right.

I had so many questions and no definitive answers, but there was still the matter of Steve and Sabrina's party. I must have jinxed it. I went home and got changed for their party and I kept an eye on my phone like a hawk watching its prey. It buzzed. I grabbed it before it could finish delivering its notification, which just so happened to be a news alert. No messages from Dr. Chris, indicating that she had changed her mind.

Like a sad soul, I drove to Steve and Sabrina's house without my plus one and sat in their driveway before going inside. I caught Steve's attention while I was still in the truck and shook my head so he knew that Dr. Chris wasn't going to be joining us tonight. I must have looked like a sad puppy. Sabrina met me at the door hugged me extra tightly.

"What's wrong, Charlie?" she asked.

"I don't know," I told her.

"Tell me what happened," she said before guiding me into their living room and listening intently to my story of everything that had led up to this point. I sat on their window seat, watching Jax play, telling her about what happened while my heart felt like it was carrying a 25 pound weight.

Sabrina's intuition kicked in. "She saw you,

Charlie."

"Yeah, I thought she saw me. At least that's what she -"

"No. Charlie, did you call her before you went to see Oakley?" Sabrina was trying not to point the question as though I had made chess moves that trapped myself, but that's exactly what I felt.

"No. I didn't need to," I told her, certain that Dr. Chris would understand why I went.

"She told you that she got extra lunch and cider, right?" Sabrina asked.

"Yes." I had just told her that and didn't understand why she was asking me about it.

"Charlie, where does she get cider?" Sabrina was guiding me to the answers to all of my questions.

"Well, WE get cider at the Fresh Grind," I told her.

Sabrina's face told me that she knew and was about to deliver the gotcha. "When you met her there that night, what did she order?"

"A cup of cider with a spoonful of sugar

plums." I paused, still missing her point.

Sabrina continued, "So she knew that they had sugarplums to put in their cider."

"Yes," I said.

"Charlie," she paused, "is that on the menu?"

"No. Oh." I had been so sullen about Dr. Chris' absence that I completely missed where Sabrina had attempted to guide me. "She's been going there for cider regularly," I said, starting to catch on. "That means, that's probably where she got her cider today."

"Yes," Sabrina said patiently.

"So she saw me and that was her way of telling me," I concluded.

"Yes," Sabrina finished.

I stood to my feet before I even knew that my brain had committed to the idea. "I gotta go, Sabrina."

"Where are you going, Charlie?" she asked with sincerity in her voice.

"To Hope Gardens. I need to see her." I

handed Sabrina their presents and turned to my Godson. "Jax, I'll see you soon, okay man? Merry Christmas!"

Steve popped his head out from the kitchen, "go get her, Charlie."

"You know it man!" I shouted in his direction, already on the move towards the front door. "Thank you, Sabrina." I hugged her once more before bounding out the door to Chief.

I took off on the way to the hospital and seemed to get stopped by the traffic lights at every intersection. It's like I was purposefully being slowed down, but I couldn't for the life of me understand why the universe, which had just worked in my favor for the last two weeks, was all of the sudden conspiring against me. After what felt like the longest drive of my life, I grabbed her gift, which I had placed in my truck just in case some miracle occurred, and ran into the lobby to see if I could find her. I hopped on the elevator, practicing what I would say to her when I saw her. The doors opened and I found my way to their floor's Family Room, hoping to catch a glimpse of her. Wish granted. There she was, in the distance, hugging a tall man who squeezed her back with excitement.

I didn't recognize the guy at all, but they

seemed to know each other very well. She kissed him on the cheek and told him how proud she was of him. My gut clinched.

"Thanks, Chris. You know I love you girl," he told her.

That was enough for me to hold my tongue. She looked so gleeful and untroubled. I wouldn't stand in her way, and I couldn't believe I was too late. Just a few hours had passed since she had seen me with Oakley. In just a few hours, she could change her mind? Maybe she had been playing me all along. But, it had all felt so real. There was no way I made this up. I thought this was different. No. I KNOW it was different. I needed a sign.

She was still hugging him. That was the affirmation that I needed. I had to let her go the same way I had let Oakley go. I was still holding her gift in my hands, but I couldn't very well go deliver it at this point. So I did what any self-respecting man who found himself standing in the face of rejection would do, I placed it on the floor beside the elevator and stepped back inside before she could see me.

Alone in the elevator I ran my hands over my face and tried to compose myself before I stepped back out into the public eye. But I could feel it there, a tightness in my chest that held my breath hostage. I hopped back in Chief and we headed towards my house.

I picked up the phone and called Steve.

"Is Sabrina near you?" I asked him.

"Yeah. Speakerphone?" he asked.

I sniffled, "Yeah. Please."

"Did you see her, Charlie?" she asked with hope in her voice.

"I did," I sniffled again.

"Oh Charlie, what happened?" Her voice sounded about as sad as I felt.

I didn't have any words, so I rode in silence for a minute, trying to compose myself.

Steve's words cut through the quietude like a knife. "I misunderstood something with Sabrina once and I almost didn't ask her about it."

"She was hugging another guy, telling him how proud she was of him," I told them. "How could I misunderstand their connection?"

"Maybe it wasn't anything, Charlie," Sabrina offered.

"He told her that he loved her, Sabrina." I sniffled again. "I left the gift for her." I paused. "I think I'm going to drive home for Christmas."

"I'm sorry man. If you want to talk, you know my number," Steve offered.

I didn't want to talk anymore, so I wrapped up all my thoughts into three simple words, "Appreciate it man."

Steve understood, "Anytime."

"Charlie?" Sabrina piped up. "Try to have an open mind, okay?"

"Yep."

I didn't want to let her go. I *knew*.

Dr. Chris:

Marlo had just told me that he got the job in Colorado. I was so proud of him for chasing his dream job, but I knew I would miss him terribly. We've been friends since the day his family moved into our neighborhood in elementary school. We survived middle and high school together and enrolled in the same undergrad and med school programs. He's helped me identify the bad fish, and I've seen him through the same, and here he was on the verge of transitioning to a place that would take him two states away. You don't get news like that about a dear friend on a regular basis, so I hugged him with all of my heart, afraid of letting go. I heard the doors of the elevator open, but I figured that we'd see whomever it was soon enough. Before I knew it, Marlo was tapping me on the shoulders. I turned around just in time to see the heels of someone stepping back onto the elevators.

"Who was it, Marlo?" I asked, thinking maybe it was a family who had gotten off on the wrong floor.

Marlo cupped the outline of his chin with his thumb and pointer finger, "I'm not sure, but he was kind of tall, maybe a couple of inches shorter than me, with brown skin and a beard with a little salt." I was impressed that he had seen all of that in such a short period of time, but there was one crucial piece of information that I was missing.

"Did he have curly hair on top?"

"Yeah," Marlo replied, "and I think he was

wearing your scarf."

Charlie. I glanced at the floor of the Family Room and noticed a package sitting beside one of the chairs near the elevator.

"Was that there before?" I asked Marlo walking over to the package.

"Was what there before?" he asked me.

I picked up the package and held it in his direction with a quizzical look on my face. "This!"

"No. I've never seen that before," he told me. He looked at the package and read the gift tag. "To my Anya, from Santa."

I gasped. "He must have seen me hugging you and left." I pulled out my phone to call him when I got paged to the Green Room.

"Marlo, can you take this to my office, please?" He nodded. "Set it on my desk so I can remember to call him when I leave the Green Room."

He grabbed the gift box from my hands, "I'll set it in there, but you know you're not going to forget."

I rushed off to the Green Room with a nagging feeling in the pit of my stomach that I must have missed something at the Fresh Grind earlier today. I greeted the patient that was in need of assistance, assessed their needs, and gave them the utmost confidence that I would do my best to help. As always, I asked the child and guardians what questions I could answer. When asked to provide a 100% guarantee that everything would be okay, I delivered the same universal truth I always shared.

"I wish I could tell you that it all ends well. Unfortunately we won't know the answer until all is said and done."

The words left my mouth headed for their family, but immediately whipped back in my direction like a boomerang, striking me in the head particularly hard. The truth was that there was no amount of protection that would guarantee I wouldn't be hurt like before. It was impossible to guard against it. Just as I was asking the family to choose where to place their hope, it was up to me to decide whether or not it was worth it to invest hope and the time it takes to get to know someone's heart. I hadn't heard him out. Instead I had cut him off like the kid who takes their ball and goes home when they don't get things their way. What's left in both of these situations is another person who has to deal with the wake of our rushed decisions. I needed to speak with Charlie, and hoped with all of my might that I wasn't too late.

As soon as the patient was taken care of, I hurried back to my office, closing the door as swiftly as I had entered. There was only a short window of time to catch Charlie so I picked up the phone and called him.

It went straight to voicemail. Actual voicemail, not his pretend version, though I wished it were him. "Hi Charlie, it's me, Dr. Chris," I paused, then clarified, "Anya. I saw that you left a package for me here at the hospital and I was hoping to catch you before you got too far away. Unfortunately, they paged me to take care of a patient before I could give you a call. Anyway, thank you for thinking of me. I don't want to open this without you. Please give me a call when you get this message or text me, something." I hung up the phone and waited with bated breath.

But I didn't receive a response, not during the rest of my shift or during the shift I picked up in avoidance.

I carted the gift home with me that night after my double shift and didn't know what to do with my anxious energy. When I stepped into the entryway I was greeted by the flowers he gave me on our first date. When I entered the living room, I was greeted by our tree Randolph, who he made me name, and had lovingly sang to as he welcomed him into our family. When I looked at the kitchen I was greeted by our dishes, which I still hadn't gotten around to washing. Everywhere I looked, I saw him. Everywhere I looked, I felt him. He was still with me, even though he wasn't present. I placed his gift underneath the tree and reminisced on every detail I could recall of the past few glorious days.

Though I had tried to do so, I failed to actually trust my gut. Instead I had let my head intercede. I knew. There wasn't any mistaking this. I knew. I just wanted another sign to confirm it. Waiting for a call that may or may not come was tough on a longing heart, so I opened my phone to bide some time. There it was, right there in my inbox. The sign. An email with the subject, "Merry Christmas from Ammons Tree Farm."

I opened the email to find a link that took me to an embedded video on their website, thanking their customers for a memorable season. I clicked play and proceeded to watch a 3 minute long montage of photos and videos of Charlie and I, picking out, cutting down, and singing to Randolph.

My heart.

I sat on the couch, not wanting to see the carnation of admiration waiting for me in my bedroom. Not knowing what else to do, I placed my phone on my heart and rested in the same spot on the couch where we had fallen asleep just a couple of nights before. His essence lingered and I thought for sure I'd have a mean sleep that night. I missed him terribly, but I feared that I would have to let him go. It certainly was not something that I wanted to do, but I couldn't hold on to an idea of what could have been.

In one final attempt to connect, I texted Charlie the link to the video. No other words accompanied it. If he didn't reply, I had my sign.

Just before I my eyelids held their nightly reunion, my phone, still resting on my chest buzzed me back to my senses. It was a text from Charlie.

"Got your voicemail. Heading to my parents' house for Christmas. Leaving tomorrow afternoon. Open the gift whenever."

"Please be careful. Will open the gift tomorrow."

And that was it. I went to sleep holding onto hope.

Chapter 14
Marley

I went to work the next day, hoping to have received another text from Charlie. But there was nothing. I went about like it was business at usual at work, but it was far from it. I was longing for Charlie, and Marlo was getting ready to leave the city as well. My body was present, but my mind was all over the place. I did the only thing I could think of to take my mind off of things. I went on my rounds and visited the children who were excited that tonight was Christmas Eve. They were all so thrilled to share with me the wishes that they had passed on to Santa at the Holiday Jubilee. It was refreshing to see, but it still kept Santa Charlie, on the forefront of my mind.

I popped in on the patient I almost lost the day after I met Charlie. I peeked around the corner to see Marley enthusiastically reading a book which made my heart leap with joy.

Knock. Knock. Knock.

Her eyes lit up as she stretched her arms out for a hug, "Dr. Chriiiiiiiiiis!!!"

"Hi Marley!" I hugged her, remembering the day of her surgery with sharp memory.

We had followed the plan methodically, and midway into surgery hit a speed bump. Marley's heart rate bottomed out. She flatlined. I closed my eyes, tilted my head back, and took a deep breath to steady my nerves. With my head still tilted back, I opened my eyes again and there she was. I was looking Marley directly in the eyes. In all of my years as a doctor, this was the first time I had an experience like that.

Her little hands cupped my face, patted my cheeks and whispered, "I know you gave your best. Remember, the rest is up to God."

I exhaled, looked back down at the table and there she was, resting peacefully while the rest of the team was talking over each other as they worked their hardest to revive her. I was overcome with peace and asked them all to be still and breathe. With all of the chaos stopped,

I rested one hand on Marley's heart, looked up at the clock in the Operating Room, and waited.

Her father's words rang out in my mind like a bell, she was going to grow up to become a young lady. I methodically called out our next steps and what I needed each member of the operating team to do. We had revived her heartbeat within 30 seconds and immediately thereafter successfully completed her surgery. It was a moment I won't soon forget. So seeing her with a book was a welcome sight for me.

"What are you reading today, Marley?" It seemed as though she had a different book for each day of the week. Today though, was the first day I saw her reading on her own.

"The Story of Santa Claus," she told me.

"Oh yeah?" I asked her. "What inspired that story?"

She looked to the door, then back at me and whispered, "I saw him."

I glanced at the door, then back and Marley and whispered, "You saw who?"

"Santa!" she said, covering her mouth at how loud she had been.

I asked when she saw Santa and listened as she told me all about the night of the Holiday Jubilee.

"My mom had stepped out to go to the bathroom and saw Santa on her way back. She asked if he would come say hi. He was the kindest man I've ever met."

"How do you know he was Santa?" I asked this bubbly, 7-year old warrior.

"I could see it in his eyes. There was a twinkle."

She was talking about Charlie. I had seen it that night too, the twinkle.

I was anxious to reconnect to Charlie through her words and experience. "Tell me more, Marley."

"Well, he asked me why I was in my room instead of in there with the rest of the children. So I told him about the surgery, and how I remembered talking to you outside of my body."

"You remember that?" I asked, more for my confirmation than for hers.

"Yeah, and when I told him about it, he asked

me how I got back into my body." She was so expressive, I felt like I was a fly on the wall.

"What did you tell him, Marley?"

An earnest look fell on Marley's face, "I told him that I watched you fight for me, and that made me want to stay." My eyes burned from the warm salty tears that were rising to the surface. She continued, "Well don't cry, Dr. Chris! It was a good story." I nodded. "Santa read me part of this book. I guess it was like an autobiography to him."

I laughed through my tears.

"He told me about the story of Santa Claus and Mrs. Claus, and how each Santa had to pick his own Mrs. Claus, so I asked if he had a Mrs. Claus yet, because he wasn't wearing a wedding ring."

Again I chuckled, "and what did he say, Marley?"

"He told me that he did, and that she was dancing with all of the other children. Which made me smile. So I asked him how he knew she was the person he was going to marry, and he told me that he just knew."

"He did?" *My heart.*

Her face lit up as she continued, "Yeah, and I could tell he believed it. So I asked him to tell me more about her, and he grinned from ear to ear as he started describing her to me."

It felt like my heart leapt through my chest. "Oh yeah?" I asked as calmly as possible.

"Yeah, Dr. Chris! I asked him if he was in love with her, and he told me that he grew more in love with her every day that he was lucky enough to spend with her."

We were like two gossiping ladies at brunch, "Santa said that!?" *Oh, this man.*

"He did, and then he asked me what my Christmas wish was, and do you know what I told him Dr. Chris?" she paused, with a hand on my shoulder, looking down on me as her eyes gazed up.

"What's that Marley?" I asked, leaning in to catch her answer.

She closed the book and sat up straight. "I told him that I wished that you would find someone who talked about you the way that Santa talked about his future wife."

I pretended I was embarrassed, “Marley!”

She giggled, “I did! I told him that, Dr. Chris.”

“You could have wished for anything for Christmas, Marley. Why was that your wish?”

“Because!” she said, looking sheepish.

“Because what, Marley?” I asked, looking at her with crossed arms and pretending like she was in trouble.

She floored me. “I’m here because your heart was so big that you wouldn’t let me go. And I wanted you to have someone in your life whose heart was so big that they would fight for you and wouldn’t let you go.”

I patted her on the hand, incapable of forming a complete thought.

“Everybody deserves that, don’t they?” she asked.

I nodded at her brilliance. “We do, Marley.”

“Whatever you do, Dr. Chris,” she said, returning to an introspective state, “you have to tell me if Santa grants my wish. He told me it would be easy to do, but I still can’t figure out how he could make a promise like that."

"I'll be sure to let you know, Marley," I told her.

"I asked him how he could promise me that and he told me that he knew your heart." *I can't.* "I mean, he is Santa, so I figured he must have been telling the truth. Plus, I can usually tell when adults are lying."

"You're a hoot, Marley."

"I know," she grinned, proud of the thought that she was considered a hoot.

"Dr. Chris?" she began, "Do you know, Santa?"

"I do," I told her.

She whispered, "Will you give him a message for me?"

"I'll try, but this is a very busy day for him, my dear."

"Will you tell him that I talked to you about this?" She looked at the doors again before continuing, "He told me not to, but I kind of wanted to know if he would grant my wish and the only way I could do that is if you knew what Santa would be bringing you for Christmas."

"I'll let him know, kiddo." I patted her hand again and nodded reassuringly in her direction. "Alright, Marley, is there anything you want to know about today?"

She was silent for the first time since I had popped into her room. She gazed at the wall beside her bed and pointed to the dove that was held up by a sticker. "Who left me this message?"

I smiled in her direction, "A young man about your age. His name is Jax."

"Do you know him too?" she asked.

"I do," I affirmed.

Still glancing at the dove Marley spoke, "Will you tell him I said thank you and that I read this every day when I wake up?"

I glanced over at his note, reading it silently, "Marley, you are a fighter. Remember you are strong even when you don't feel like it."

The tears just wouldn't leave me alone today. "I'll tell him, Marley."

"Thank you, Dr. Chris!"

"You're welcome, Marley!" I said, rising from my chair and heading towards the doorway.

"Merry Christmas!!"

Her spirit was contagious, "Merry Christmas, kiddo. Keep on reading, fighter."

"I will!" she said as I leaned back in and crossed pinkies with her. It was our promise to each other that we'd both give our best today.

I left her room and headed back to my office, texting Charlie on the way.

"Dear Santa, just spoke with Marley. She told me her Christmas wish."

His reply came swiftly. "Open your gift."

I replied, "ok."

I couldn't get back to my office fast enough. The promise of tears stung my eyes as I ran down the hallway, slid around the corner and entered my office, frantically searching for the gift that I had carried back to work with me.

Marlo caught a glimpse of my sprint and

rushed to my side, assuming something was horrifically wrong. I told him about Marley's conversation with Charlie and what he shared with her the night of the Jubilee.

"Where's the gift, Chris?" he anxiously asked me.

I placed it on the table, too faint-hearted to unwrap it.

"What are you afraid of, Chris? It's written all over your face," he asked.

"I don't know," I lied.

I was met with the look of a stern father, "If you don't unwrap it, I'm going to. Are you ready to explain that to Charlie?" *No.*

"Don't you touch it. Just give me a minute to sit with my thoughts, please. I'm trying to push through the feeling that this could be the end of everything."

Finally understanding my fear, Marlo eased up. "Stay open, Chris," he told me as he walked out of my office, leaving me seated at the desk with the gift sitting in front of me.

I took a deep breath, picked up my phone,

and added an item to our Christmas List before sending Charlie another text. "Are you still in the city?"

"Did you open it?" he replied.

I sent honesty back his way, "No."

Which was met with confusion, "???"

I two-thumbed my explanation as quickly as I could, while I knew he was receptive to it, "I need to see you before I open this, Charlie."

"I'm about to leave, Chris." Maybe he wasn't as receptive as I thought.

I clarified further, "I just want to talk to you before you go."

There was no reply. I waited for the next 20 minutes before assuming he was on the road headed to his parents house. Sensing that there wasn't going to be a reply, I placed my hands on the gift from Charlie and slowly unwrapped the paper, to find a lidded box. Tears still filled my eyes as I placed both hands on top of the lid, and asked for the strength to lift the cardboard when I heard the words of Marley ringing in my head, "I wanted you to have someone in your life whose heart was so big that they would fight for you and wouldn't let you go."

I inhaled deeply and held my breath as I peered inside the box and read the handwritten note resting atop the tissue paper, "To my Anya, I'll fight for you for as long as there is breath in my lungs. - Santa"

My exhale turned on the waterworks, which warmed my cheeks as tears flowed from my eyes.

At that point, I didn't care what was inside the box. I only wanted to see Charlie. But he wasn't there and the gift inside was all I had of him. I lifted the note from the box and was just about to peel back the tissue paper to reveal the gift when I was paged over the hospital intercom. I fully heard Susan's voice, and I know I worked at a hospital, but I couldn't will myself to get up from my chair until I saw his gift. Hurriedly, I moved the tissue paper to the side to find a pewter disc with a red ribbon threaded through a hole in the top. My face crumpled as I looked closer and discovered that the gift inside was a stethoscope ornament. I gingerly lifted it out of the box and ran my fingers over the raised design. Feeling something on the other side, I turned it over to find an inscription, "For Anya, to hang on every Randolph we find. Love, Santa." I wept, but only had a breath to enjoy the moment before I was paged again.

"Paging Dr. Chris to the Family Room. Dr. Chris to the Family Room."

That wasn't Susan's voice. I stepped out of my office, tears in my eyes, knowing that unmistakable, deep, raspy voice.

I walked towards the Family Room at a fervent pace, racing towards the man in the scarf, my scarf.

"Charlie?" I asked, hoping my eyes and ears had not deceived me.

He had been speaking with Marlo, but turned around to face me, a look of relief washed over him. The twinkle was still in his eyes and his grin resurfaced as he spoke, "I came as soon as I could, but I stopped to get you something." He held up two ciders, each with a spoonful of sugarplums, the last thing I added to the list.

Marlo grabbed the ciders from Charlie's hands, completely freeing him to envelop me in a warm, spinning, embrace. There we were in the hallway, in front of visiting families, in front of staff, in front of Marley's room, gifting ourselves the grace of two healing hearts.

He lowered me to the ground, exhaling with ardor, before wiping the tears from my cheeks and placing his forehead on mine.

"Charlie, I-"

He interjected before I could speak, "Marlo, told me."

A million thoughts flooded my mind, but only one word came out, "Oakley?"

"I told her to stop calling me." I found myself fighting for air. "Come with me today?" he asked.

My heart. I nodded as quickly as I'd heard his question.

"Yes?" he asked me. I nodded again. "Yes?"

"Yes, Charlie," I breathed into his ear.

Marley squealed with delight as she watched her Christmas wish come true. Charlie swayed with me in the hallway as he hummed the beginning of The Little Christmas Tree. I used my hands to trace the outline of his beard before singing the second verse aloud to him.

"Promise you will be
Nobody else's little Christmas Tree

I'll make you sparkle, just you wait and see
My little Christmas Tree"

He kissed me with the intense earnestness that was reserved for love, and I owe it all to a spoonful of sugarplums.

The Start of Something New

Acknowledgements

With sincere gratitude for always encouraging my wild ideas, I thank my parents. There will never be enough words to express my appreciation for all you've done to encourage my growth.

To my closest friends, who pushed me through writer's doubt, I thank you for reminding me that a draft is the start of something great.

To LaNeé Bridewell, Sophia Garcia, Larry Hunt, Kelly Jones, Rita Prior, and JeT'aime Taylor, the fabulous Beta Readers who provided me with the feedback that pushed me through the completion of this draft, you'll never understand just how valuable your thoughts truly were.

Lastly, to my husband, Herston, who prepared food and replenished drinks before I even knew I needed them, thank you for supporting me on this wild journey. I was able to finish this in such short time in part because of you.

About the Author

C. L. Fails is an Author, Creative Architect, and an Accidental Educator; having served pre-school through college students in her hometown of Kansas City. An agent for equity, she has dedicated her career to helping others learn to follow their internal compass, and thrive despite challenge. Cynthia is currently Founder & CEO of LaunchCrate Publishing - a company created to help writers launch their work into the world while retaining the portion of profit they deserve. Outside of LaunchCrate she is an active advocate for education, serving as a former Girls on the Run Coach, on the Board of Directors for the Children's Campus of Kansas City, on the K-State in KC Task Force, as well as Chair Emeritus of the Multicultural Alumni Council at Kansas State University.

She is author and illustrator of the Ella Book Series, The Christmas Cookie books, and her latest series, "The Secret World of Raine the Brain." She also penned the interactive modern memoir, "So, Okay..." documenting the life stories of her then 94 year old Grandfather. All are fun books that inspire us to be bold, take risks, and learn from our mistakes. When she's not helping clients, hosting a podcast, speaking with audiences or working on her latest book about building community, you can find her doodling on whatever object may be nearby.

CPSIA information can be obtained
at www.ICGtesting.com
Printed in the USA
FSHW022114160120
65992FS